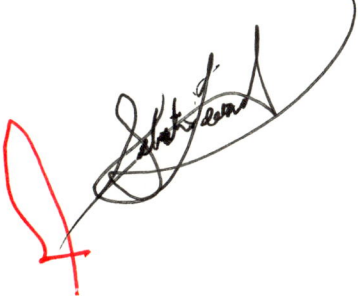

A Draemorian Chronicle

The Western World

This is a freely distributed copy of the self-published novel. Please pass this on to the next friend or family member when you've finished.

To obtain a professionally edited and published copy of the novel, please pre-order and register by e-mail at:

https://www.inkshares.com/projects/a-draemorian-chronicle-the-western-world

Part of the Fated Series

Written by Sebastien Leonard

Illustrated by Derek Sproule

Copyright © 2014

Kirkus Reviews

Tracking centuries of history across multiple civilizations, Leonard's debut novel entangles forces angelic, demonic, and technological into a skein of interlinked short stories and journal entries.

Sorrownote is a wandering minstrel, and the various chapters of this book are either excerpts from his journals or stories he's collected as part of his travels. Characters such as Caelith Bearspaw and the witch Moranda narrate chapters on the history of the lands of Draemoria. These historical sketches outline the Angelic Kingdom of Elysica and demonic Dornar, as well as the battle-torn Blood Plains, the island of Paradigm, and the peaceful haven of Belliscia. The first two-thirds of the book detail the lands and history, while the final third, a novella, recounts the events of the Blood Plains War. Joseph, a young man of Belliscia, is transformed into a demon, then, that same night, he meets the mysterious Jennifer, who may or may not be as much angel as he is demon. Together, they set out to solve the mystery of Joseph's transformation, along the way finding themselves caught up in events that are drawing to a head on the Blood Plains. War threatens, and it may take the entire world with it, unless Joseph and Jennifer can work together to stop it. The story of the Blood Plains War, however, isn't as strong as the imagination that went into creating the varied lands of Draemoria. It's readily apparent that a great deal of quality thought went into creating this world and the philosophical underpinnings that support it. Unfortunately, so much attention is paid to the world's history that character and plot suffer. Many character voices are indistinguishable from the surrounding narration, particularly in the early historical chapters. Benneth Aldercaine is an exception. His plotline interacts well with his history—he's part demon/human/Elysican—which complicates his intriguing fate.

Imaginative fantasy, but the history often weighs down, rather than supports, its characters.

About The Author

Sebastien Leonard is a geomatic/civil engineering analyst and plan draftsman with a lifelong aspiration of producing a single cohesive, complex, and fantastic environment to deliver messages on many subjects by utilizing one seamless storyline.

Over fifteen years of writing, this story has evolved from several short stories into an involved plot, spanning a series of five genre-diverse novels in a world unlike any other. It is the author's intention to cross media platforms into film and video games in an effort to tackle world issues, concepts, and misperceptions. He has also prepared scripts, game concepts, and hired concept artists and illustrators in an attempt to perpetuate this ambition.

Sebastien is a descendant of several of the oldest French Canadian bloodlines who landed in Canada as early as 1582. He had been born on a military base and raised in English-speaking Canada, moving thirty times in his life to date. He pursued a career in engineering for an opportunity to change his world physically. In his personal adventures he had witnessed many different aspects of Canadian culture which became a catalyst of inspiration for his novels.

The Western World

The Eastern World

The Hall of Great Kings

The Great Tower

The Pantheon War

Contents

Preface 1

Prologue 2

The Tribal Land of the Blood Plains 16

The Demonic Kingdom of Dornar 41

Paradigm, Island of Ash 72

Belliscia, Island of Serenity 84

The Angelic Kingdom of Elysica 90

The Blood Plains War 124

    Chapter 1 124

    Chapter 2 141

    Chapter 3 152

    Chapter 4 164

    Chapter 5 178

    Chapter 6 189

    Chapter 7 196

Preface

If you are reading this story, it is either because I, Sorrownote, have handed down this literature for future generations, have been found dead, or because you are one of many whose soul has continued to live on this planet through to the end of time. In my opinion, this must be the aspiration of all great writers. Not just to leave a legacy or an interesting story for future generations or even civilizations. To have their words live to the end of time.

On this note, I will begin with an introduction to the wisdom you are about to receive. I first began writing this story as a journal, a woeful ballad of regret and loss, a requiem to what may have been, and a fool's hope at bringing justice into the darkest places. As my story progressed and as I witnessed greater things that shaped those ever small events I had taken on so personally, I realized the gravity of my writing. It was once a selfish attempt at shaping my world and became a selfless attempt at changing our world for the greater good of all its inhabitants.

Along my journeys I have written several books which form our "Draemorian Chronicle". A few of these books have been written on the travels alongside my cherished friends, and the others have been written under the guidance of those with wisdom far beyond mine.

At the beginning of every book, I have introduced the inspired authors and their respective civilizations. From there on, you will have the opportunity to enjoy two hundred years of their flourishing, leading to our present day. Afterward, you will find my narrated and ongoing chronicle which I have called "The Blood Plains War".

Before we begin, I would like to share our story to give you understanding of how and why our world exists the way it is. This story is a story that all inhabitants of Draemoria continue to share to their children.

Prologue

At the beginning, before all of this greatness and tragedy, there was a tribe of nomads who roamed the plains, hunted its animals and pulled the grain from their stalks. They never took more than they needed from their land, for the less they destroyed, the more it would grow.

Their children would play on the river banks, and when the season was right, they would climb in the mountains searching for new trails in sheer zest of exploration.

There came a day in this first of tribes, their three most respected wise men sat around a fire. Their conversation was simple and clear.

They began a discussion of how all things came into being.

The wise man favouring darkness claimed, "The universe must have been created from darkness. Darkness can exist without light, and must have existed before light came into being. It must be the source of all things. Darkness is where true power lies."

The wise man favouring light responded, "I disagree. From light comes life and prosperity. Even if darkness can live in absence of light, life cannot. Darkness is void of power. Light must be the source of all creation."

The wise man in favour of evidence, clearly uninterested then stated, "I think this discussion is ridiculous. If the universe is so vast, time must be equally as vast. Who can say, from one single life, that any of our claims are absolute? Running off on childish perceptions will not aid the future of our people."

As their discussion continued it turned to argument. It seemed the fire itself began to take shape, favoring light, darkness, and sheer heat. The leaders, incapable of reaching an agreement, stood before the people and forced them to choose sides. At that moment they divided the people and went their ways. Only the few who would not choose sides remained.

The wise man who felt the light carried one quarter of the people to the north, among the flood plains rich in life and wild fields, where they may be adequately nurtured by the light.

The wise man who felt darkness brought his quarter of followers south to the swamps, where the treacherous environment was no match for the greatness the darkness would provide them.

The wise man who was complete without so-called "power from beyond" and without circumstance brought the third quarter in disbelief into the mountains were they would amass great resource.

Then, there were those who remained in the fields, uninterested in any claim. They became known as the Blood Plains Tribe and continued to be the descendants of the first tribe.

As time passed, the ideals of two minds became worship and unquestioning belief. One day a doorway in their temples opened. Beings from beyond their world stepped through.

In the Temple of Light, a gateway to the heavens opened. Angels entered our world and taught the truth to the people. Their unquestioning faith and belief had bestowed upon them a saving grace. In their modesty and lack of understanding, they had been blessed with a love as a Father to his children. In this miraculous event, the angels decided to reside as a governing body, teaching growth, prosperity, domestication and agriculture to the people. Other casts were made in resourcefulness such as hunters, gatherers, tinkers and tradesmen. Above all other teachings, the Word of Truth was then taught to the people, nurturing their souls with the Virtues of life and love.

In the Temple of Darkness, a bottomless pit leading to the abyss came forward and reeked of deception and fear. Demons crawled out of the hole speaking untold lies of vanities and lusts to be gained, and sin to be satisfied. They taught the people of horrible things that could feed their lust and ambitions. In turn, selfishness and sacrifice became a lifestyle. The world of the swamp became a chaotic chain of parasitic chaos, feeding on each other's wealth and health to the point of death.

For some reason beyond their knowing, they found that they were now victim to mortality. Not only were they able to pair with humans and have offspring, but they were also capable of dying from age and fatality. A truce had been called between their kings to meet once more and discuss this peril. They met with the wise man within Mechanus to resolve this troubling issue.

The wise man spent his days attempting to disprove the futile claims of his kin and built a portal device. His antithesis was: if such a device would never succeed, then existence must be as it is simply perceived. Unfortunately, his device did work and the portal bridged to a world called Mechanus. Mechanus was a world that had devoted its efforts to developing an artificial intelligence two millennia ago. This intelligence soon covered the planet and became one massive construct, and in turn one being. Its residences became blood to the arteries. After an age it began embracing life and the living, and craved its own soul. It now has been attempting to find its way to other worlds. It began pouring through the portal and soon following expanded the portal complete with control pads to other dimensions and a built-in coffee maker. It began taking on the tribe as its blood vessels, installing crystals into their bodies that would link them to the source. This level of "belonging" gave the wise man a great feeling of presence beyond the unbelievable metaphysical, that all answers could be attained through what exists.

The wise man then claimed, "Well look at you all. I guess my brothers were right. And here I was, trying to prove you all wrong. Wow. Angels and demons, huh? I'm surprised you're all so old... and feeble..."

The archangel responded, "I don't know how to explain this, but we are dying. We don't die. We live forever. Can you explain what is happening to us?"

"Well, I can't, but I'm sure someone around here is. Do you see that? I was trying to disprove your existence. This thing wasn't even supposed to work. Out of a sudden, it opens on its own. I couldn't believe my eyes, then these things began pouring out and altering the world. One of them explained to me that they were just blood cells of the greatest organism of all time named "Mechanus" and they are seeking its soul. They didn't really give me an option of refusal, but who cares. Have you ever tasted coffee? They even installed a coffee maker directly into the portal."

The devil burst out, "We know about this world, we know about all worlds. What is happening to us?"

The wise man, clearly unamused turned to the devil. "Wow. My first moment of glory and it's all 'me, me, me'. Fine. Give me a second."

At that moment, he turned to what appeared to be a high ranking official of the Mechanoid community and requested "Fetch me a solution."

The Mechanoid then stepped through the portal, and a crystal on the back of its head shimmered. Within moments, a helicopter carrier landed on the other side of the portal and a representative stepped through into their plane.

The representative answered, "I will aid you, but the circumstances of your fates may span generations. If I do, you must promise me this: I will rule your land for all time. Not as a functioning body of government, but to maintain a balance that would keep you from destroying yourselves."

The leaders agreed to his demands, at which point he explained, "You are from immortal planes. Being immortal and without time was one of the governing mechanics of where you are from. We have been witnessing, here and in other planes, life crossing between planes adapts and conforms to the mechanics of the destination. That being said, now that you live in a mortal plane where death and decay is a natural occurrence and a mechanic of this universe, you are all now mortal. Not just mortal as in you may die, but you are also decaying on a cellular level, aging, and eventually you will die."

From that point forward, the representative decided to study the land, and found that there were islands beyond the mainland. He discovered the island of Belliscia which appeared to be a cornucopia of sustained life, the island of Paradigm which was made from ash and cinder and populated by ferocious beasts, and an island called The Hall Of Great Kings where a being who called himself the War Lock claimed that he had lived for all time in order to settle conflicts between nations. After finding all these new peculiar facts, he decided to build a tower in the southernmost mountain ranges in order to overlook everything. At the end of the generation, the representative called for the respective leaders once more to divulge his knowledge.

"My first question upon my arrival was 'what is in this world beyond what they already know?' and so I investigated for myself," said the representative, "and so I traveled by my own means beyond your horizons and found several islands surrounding this massive island.

"I also took note that these islands could see these mountains as clear as day, and took reference to this perching you sit in now." A slight mutter of pride escaped his lips. "So in turn I intend to put these islands to use, one of which is already in use as you can see by the great walls and keep contained.

"Now I am going to spell everything out for you now and all the things I am about to say must be made clear to your peoples. These will be carried beyond your bones and the bones of your descendants.

"I have been aware of a population unaccepting the newfound fate of your land. They wish to live as things were, uninhibited by what you proclaim to give them. These people will be granted amnesty from your beliefs and granted that island to the northwest, named Belliscia. As you can see, it is completely self-sufficient and has a dock prepared in times of drought, famine or sickness.

"There is also a band of nomads that claim the right to their land, and refuse to move to the island. I have found a way to solve their problem while solving a problem of my own. The free roaming wild fields that separates Dornar and Elysica, which for the moment only exists because you have not expanded that far, will now be called The Blood Plains and remain in possession of the nomads. If a war is called between your sides it will be fought on the Blood Plains and not on civilian soil. The nomads claim the right to the land, and so killing a nomad will be a direct violation of the laws and grounds for immediate death. If the nomads take a side, it is their right to you as it is to all things in their land. If they win, you will die. If you win, you will be destroyed.

"Whether you believe it or not, and this concept may be beyond you, but your angels and demons are now finding love and offspring with human counterparts. What amazes me is how your people have managed to bear compatible genetics, but that is beyond the point. Angel and demon blood will cross but not directly. All though your species have a conflict down to the very fibre of your existences, your half offspring's blood has been paired with mortal blood and in that has found crossover. I have not experimented or tested such a thing and what the effects may be, but if my calculations are correct, they may be unstable, and may become more than just a nuisance for either side. If such a child is born, they will be called chaosbloods and casted to that island to the southwest which I have dubbed Paradigm, for their existence is a paradigm and could be catastrophic to the balance we are trying to maintain. This land is a swell of ash and cinders created from the bubbling of a fault line. What does live there, lives there by its own ingenuity. Such an environment would be beneficial in preventing an escape and in turn evading turmoil.

"The final island, to the northeast, has been called the Hall of Great Kings. Why do I say 'it has been called' and not 'I have called'? Well, I cannot explain this, but when I discovered this island, everything on it had already existed. Whole fields of graves with a great keep on its northern cliffs, and a field beyond its walls where weapon and armor alike are still donned by skeletons or remains of such.

"This Hall had an occupant and to my surprise had welcomed me with open arms. He called himself the War Lock. He claims the soul of a sided king who falls to Absolution. He also knew about this day I am presenting to you. He had a claim of his own for you, and his words are of life and death, so listen clearly.

The representative begins to read a scroll:

'I am the War Lock, and my purpose is as follows:

In times of war, there are some wars that seem to never end. These wars in truth can lead to complete genocide and death to all who become involved. To prevent this, my existence is clear: To call for Absolution.

When I see fit, the world will be filled with a bellowing sound of trumpets. This trumpet is the call for the Battle of Absolution. The two kings in argument have ten days to respond with their finest hundred soldiers. If they do not respond, the land will fill with plague and all life will die slowly and horribly. When they arrive on my island, both sides will be given two days upon arrival of the latest team to prepare for battle. The battle will go as follows. There is only one victory: When one King falls. The remaining king will have his way in any dispute which ignited said war and the soldiers will return to their homes. The fallen king will then be brought into my Halls to rest in peace.'

"With that said, I believe you should all think deeply on your decisions in war, for they may be fatal, especially as king."

*****

Journal Entry,

A gentle and yet woeful experience this life has become. I, Sorrownote of the Wolf's Howl Tribe, come from a long line of proud and nomadic hunters, living in the graces of our noble land and free from regulation and persecution. Today, rules pit us between two civilizations bound in insufferable spite, ravaging our lands over simple spits and continue to prosper without decency for those who they have trampled asunder. But we live on. Day by day we reclaim our land. Day by day we yield its fruits with wisdom gained from those who prosper. Not to cultivate or engineer, but to rebuild what had been lost so we may continue on our chosen path.

As a child I remember travelling with my parents and sister Syrenne. Now she was not kin by blood, but kin by tribe. She belonged to the Eagle's Eyes, and her parents died a few seasons ago from sickness. Sickness was one thing we never held bitterness against. It was part of our way of life and it was natural.

I remember travelling with my parents and Syrenne as a band of ruthless half-demons called Dornarians ravaged our supplies, our steeds, and even our parents in the process. Demonic folk have never held back on an easy conquest. Syrenne and I hid in a bog among the tall grass where our scent would be submerged in filth.

I remember it taking years to take hold of my sanity, my sister fending for me as I would barely act or even speak for my own survival. It was one fateful day when a minstrel witnessed my sister feeding me and decided to break camp with us that I would reclaim myself.

This minstrel was named Vardacoire, and he must have been the greatest musician to have ever graced my ears. After a night of soft lullabies, and a morning of bountiful provision, he had offered us the opportunity to learn as his disciples. For years, we followed him endlessly until we mastered the gifts he had freely given us.

Along our journeys, we had endless discussions of the fates of our world, why things are the way they are and why we must endure the events we endure. His teachings always led to the conclusion that if we do not endure, we will no longer exist. Our world will become a shade of an old people long since passed, and there will be no recollection of who we are. Angels and demons will conquer and cover our lands with their respective utopian ideals, until they converge and collapse on each other. Then all will be lost.

I did not share his perspectives. I question why they ever had to exist in the first place. Why did they ever come into our land? Not so much the angels, for they brought forth prosperity and held high the authority of rules and justice, but demons. Why should demons also be given like rights? And by this I formed an unethical conclusion. I was hell bent on satisfaction. I became immersed in a twisted ideal of natural justice. The demons will pay for their faults.

After Vardacoire had passed we claimed heir to his possessions. They were not many, excepting the finest instruments in the land. I had always favoured the lute. There was something about playing a variety of complex chords with the frills of well keyed prime chords that my soul savoured. Syrenne preferred the pan pipes for their whimsical melodies, but also enjoyed the hand harp.

We decided to become minstrels for the land. Our purpose would be to share the news between the tribes and warn them of areas that had been ravaged by our neighbours. Our music had been embraced, and the people utilized it to plan ambushes and assaults on our assailants. The Blood Plains Tribe began to rebuild its strength to defend its land.

It was then I began writing this journal, and as we passed from land to land, I wrote letters that would introduce its content. I decided to speak to one of our wisest councilmen on the matter, so I figured a taste of my knowledge would be best suited for its introductory letter.

Long ago, our ancestors lived as we do, free from these civilizations, and it was good. It was peace and it was free. We chose to continue on our path, not knowing the worlds our kin had committed into our own, and we continued to choose our path because it had been our path to choose.

Over time, conflict arose between the neighbours. This conflict was not stewed by our kin. No, our kin still had a love for each other, even beyond their petty differences. They now had allies, and they were not from this world. Apparently our neighbours became so involved in their beliefs that they had managed to open gates to the heavens and hells, angels and demons now resided among them.

The angels of the north were illustrious, both in form and in presence. They began bringing into the world concepts of virtue and invested in the people's skills and talents. Every action they made was out of love, and our neighbours flourished. Of all these graces, they had one resentful attitude. There was no room for demons in their world. The angels seemed to ignore the rules of the borders, not to the point of infringing on our rights to the land or to self-rule, but to provide us with some of this knowledge in order to replenish what may be taken from us by the demons. As a neighbour they lived in regret over what they must do on our land to preserve their way of life so they enjoyed aiding us and helping us to rebuild our homes.

The demons of the south were vile. How could one want to live amongst such creatures? Stories crossed our paths of sadistic, parasitic chaos and destruction in the name of vanity. The swamp itself quivered in fear. Yet through all of this vileness, the civilization continued to expand within the swamps, decimating its resources in greed and foolishness. I can see why the angels had no place for demons, and yet the angels obeyed the laws of the land for it was the swamp dwellers' choice to live the way they lived, laying in the bed they had created for themselves. I also feel that the angels would have been more selfless in their resolve if they were not mortal.

The pain and sadness gripped the people of the north, and they began to cross the plains. Over generations, many battles had been fought in an attempt to weaken their enemy, but the demons continued to pour out of their abyss, breeding with the human population and running rampant in the maledict swamps.

At some point in our history, Mechanus became involved. The representative who sat in a tower atop the highest peaks in the eastern lands had been aware of these tribulations, and called forth leaders from all sides. He stated that The Blood Plains had been intended as a battle field and nothing more, and the Blood Plains Tribe still claimed right over the land. He also stated that the people would be left alone or their adversaries would be met with absolute resolve, utterly destroying the assailant.

At that time, we had no idea how the representative would manage to stand behind his claim, but then it happened. Mechanoids began filing down from the mountains with great caravans reinforced with plates of steel. They had no steeds but were releasing dark clouds of smoke and made indistinguishable noises. The Mechanoids themselves were heavily armoured, almost as if there was no man bearing it. The armour itself seemed far too cumbersome for men their size, and even great men would have trouble supporting their frame, let alone traversing mountain paths.

The lead of the Mechanoids came bearing gifts of weapons and armour. They even provided provisions that would long outlast what we currently utilized, such as tents with indestructible canvasses. At first, our leaders were refusing the gifts, but then the Mechanoids assured us that it would not change our way of life or even how we viewed combat. They would provide no advanced tools or weaponry. They simply wished to re-engineer the quality of our life with much more suitable equipment to aid our existence amongst our neighbours.

Unfortunately, after an age, the Mechanoids never returned. Their gear became dull and their provision became rendered useless under the constant battering by the seasons and the neighbours. Even with provision from a great technological nation such as Mechanus, The Blood Plains was doomed to destruction.

Because of all of this, The Blood Plains only lived a vacant memory of their once embraced nomadic life. They now lived in fear of their neighbours, favouring their knowledge of overlooked terrain, hunting when they can, and hiding when they could not. Unfortunately war was not the only pestilence on their land. Since Dornar relished in anarchy and they crossed the border for flesh the swamps could not supply. They continued to attack and blunt against Mechanus' provided might. Unfortunately for us the gear was not indestructible and their persistence eventually whittled our defense. We became vulnerable once more. We then lived in fear.

Even with all this war and hatred, we had never heard the "Trumpets of Absolution" sound. Every petty battle was insignificant and held no bearing of long term consequence. Most of its fault came from the ravaging south and the healing north. They would have their battles, lives would be lost, and then it would end. We would attempt to reclaim our land by destroying or burying the remains. The battles became too much and our fathers began to give up. They decided to leave the land asunder, for the land, even repaired, would not exist in its natural state any longer. They had repaired the land to the extent that it no longer resembled their home. They realized that this is their home now, and they would live with it.

As of late, in our generation, the sundering had become more regular. The demons appear starved and desperate, and the angels become more adamant in their resolve. Day after day, attacks between our neighbours became a common occurrence. We are grateful for their persistence, but the conflict never ends. When they recede, the demons have their way with the land and we fall victim of their crimes.

And this is how our land came to be.

*****

The Tribal Lands of the Blood Plains

The Tribal Land of the Blood Plains

I am Caelith Bearspaw of the Bear's Paw Tribe. If you are reading this story, then you can account for the wisdom that is about to be bestowed upon you. Sorrownote is one of our most gifted children and had requested an audience with me as I am the most invested in the history of our people. Please, listen to these words, for they are the fruit of human nature.

Our people lived in this land since time before time, embracing the sunlight, relaxing in the moonlight, and travelling anywhere we pleased. The north, south and even east had been our home once and each of them held their own essence to beauty that made this world breathtaking. We above all knew every inkling and fabric that made this world our home and delighted in all the fruits it had to offer.

We were one with its trees, its grass and its flowers. We were also one with its deer, its wolf and its bear. We ran alongside horses and dug with the gophers. Every life, no matter how large or small, was part of us down to our very spirit. In a time not so long ago, we were kin to their spirits and we would seek their council for guidance. The noble bear taught us of protection. The wolves taught us unity, camaraderie and the importance of family. From these animals we learned to invoke the spirits within ourselves.

We also learned the plants of this world also contained spirits, for they provided us with nourishment, medicine, vision, and even clothing. In time, we learned that animals would give their lives so we may feed, and learned of the nourishment gained from the flesh of things. In respects for their spirit and the spirits of their kin we would use bone and skin for tools and clothing, leaving nothing unused.

We then began to speak to the animals and honed our first language. Our language was built on communication with the spirits, and through our spirits we learned to speak to each other. In that respect, our language was a language of the spirit which would be known as the Spirit Tongue. Some among us were more adept at this concept, and became our wise men. It had been placed on their shoulders to teach the people of this knowledge and the wisdom it could share over time. Entire generations went on this way, even to this day, passing knowledge down in the spirit tongue from father to son.

Sitting around a campfire, our wise men began making drawings that would discuss locations within our land that were fruitful for different resources. In this art they expanded the knowledge of their respective tribes through sharing. Art became a new cornerstone for our culture, so even those incapable of the spirit tongue could leave knowledge for their children.

When watching the bear, we saw how it would trample and mark trees to mark its land. No predator dared to enter the bear's domain. We learned that the bear's paw was an iconic symbol of protection. We began imprinting bear's paw prints in the ground around our camps, and the spirit of the bear would protect us from the night hunting beasts.

There were night hunting beasts, and many of them would kill and eat a man given the opportunity, but we understood them. They did not hate us or attack us out of spite. They hunted us in the natural order of things as we had learned to attack the boar. We grew a respect for all forms of beast. Even those who wished to kill us. We believed their purpose in our life was to hone our prowess, to challenge and test us.

Among our warriors it was an honour to be compared to the night beasts, for no beast during the day could match their cunning. It was then that men began to be divided from each other, and our people built tribes based on the spirits who gifted them.

We started with ten tribes. Each tribe had been given respect to their spirit animal. Those who were born of a tribe and gifted with another would marry into that tribe and become one of theirs.

The Deer's Horn was the most dominant of tribes. Although they shared very little skill, they had an affinity for rule. Their knowledge was based on the presence and location of all their tribes and their condition. They set themselves aside to monitor and unite the people. Among each other they were constantly in argument for who would lead.

The Wolf's Howl had a knack for unity and territory. They had the ability to call out over long distances, to message or to warn others. They were one of the first tribes to embrace language for the wolves spoke often and clearly.

The Gopher's Claw loved the dirt and rocks. From the rocks they had found ore which would produce metals. In later times they would become our smiths and stoneworkers, and were capable of shaping our terrain.

The Eagle's Eye had great and unparalleled sight. They travelled regularly with the Wolf's Howl for they could foresee attacks from predators and incoming disasters. In time they would be our first line of defense from our neighbours, and with education became archers.

The Bear's Paw became the defenders. They were not quite as skilled at combat as the Stalker's Fang, but they had a great resilience and were capable of fortifying with any material at their disposal. Their sigils would offer great protection, and any who were protected by the Bear's Paw Tribe usually went unchallenged.

The Horse's Mane lived as the symbol of freedom. Of all the tribes, they were the most free spirited and would roam the lands to no end. They were the most impossible to keep track of, even for Eagle's Eye. They became adventurers and would travel to the farthest corners of our land.

The Stalker's Fang were the most cunning of all the tribes. They had been found to be warrior elites, capable of vanquishing any and all enemies. They embraced the darkness above all, as it was an invaluable tool.

The Rabbit's Foot was the most gentle of our tribes. They lived alongside the smaller creatures, and became great herb gatherers and enjoyed eating solely of vegetation. They also had a gift for providing sustenance to the other tribes, especially in times of need such as the winter seasons, and providing healing remedies from rare herbs that would save lives on countless occasions.

The Beaver's Tail loved the forest. They had learned of the great architecture that lumber would provide and with the lumber managed to create permanent structures that would allow the tribe to find shelter. They also learned to hone their abilities to prepare equipment and facilities that would propel the other tribes in their endeavours. Down the road they would commonly work with the Gopher's claw for metals and stones that would advance their design.

The Sheep's Fleece found utility in our land animals. Eventually they would learn how to make clothing and fineries. The fineries then had been advanced with dyes, and embroidery would be made in the clothing that would allow the people to be unique. It had also been found that the people who had clothing rather than leathers were less prone to sickness, and they worked alongside the Rabbit's Foot to advance their holistic remedies.

Among these tribes, a tribunal had been formed of the greatest wise men to rule over all the tribes in order to maintain the unity beyond reasonable doubt. They would hold traditional celebrations that would call our people together, and on those days our children would join their spirit tribe. The tribunal would also call for any major cause of distress among the people, so that they could be accounted for as a whole. This would include devastation, travelling predators, natural disasters, or even outside influences if they ever occurred. They had no call for exiles or traitors, for there was a strong unity within the people and no one ever questioned each other's loyalties.

All the tribes saw what we had created for ourselves and saw that it was good and we all lived in harmony, at least until that fateful day.

During our summer solstice, all the tribes would meet in the forest bordering the mountains, dance around the fires and tell stories. Three of our wise men sat alone. They began a discussion that erupted into an argument, and in that argument were adamant on dividing our people apart. It was the darkest day in our history, for many families had been torn apart.

Many of our family would head to the north where the flood plains would bring them life. Many went to the south were the darkness would develop their cunning. Many went to the east to amass great resource. There were no specific tribes that chose sides, mind you. It was as if the people were divided by heart and spirit rather than by their ambitions. Even the most obvious Stalker's Fang was divided, and many of them stayed within the plains or went north to protect their more docile kin.

After the separation, our ancestors decided that a tribunal of leaders was not enough. A simple argument had divided our people for all future generations, and we no longer had control over what fate had in store from us. So, it was decreed that from this point on a council will rule over the tribe and make decisions only based on absolute agreements. Any discussion to reach an ambiguous verdict would be held stale until the verdict had been reached.

The Blood Plains Council began with ten members. Each member being the elder of a family's branch of the tribe, in turn providing representation from all the nomadic tribes within the plains. Every tribe was informed of the location of the council regularly, and the council itself became its own nomadic commune.

It was almost as if our kin sided against each other. They would no longer speak to each other and even after our attempts to speak would end up in futile arguments that would divide the discussion. They would get upset and leave. Later, they even refused to speak with us, for we were 'lukewarm' in our convictions. The council decided if our neighbours did not want to speak to us, we would no longer speak to them.

In the first generation, the council had decreed the tribes would bound their land fairly, favouring the natural features of the plains and creating monuments of stone that would delineate ownership of land between the Blood Plains and their neighbours. Over time, the monuments became insignificant as the neighbouring land began to take form by the influence of their inhabitants. The civilizations began to flourish, and yet the Blood Plains remained untouched.

Eagle's Eye caught a visage one day. They saw men with wings soaring in the distance. Over the flood plains they had eagle wings, and they became intrigued. Over the swamps they saw bat wings, and it made them cower. Eagle's Eye approached their council member who would then inform the council of this information. It was decided they would investigate.

Proud and noble, Deer's Horn crossed the northern boundary and into the flood plains. After a long journey across the flood plains and toward these flying men, they had seen a sight they would never forget. It was as if the grains had been marching single file, and the animals had been sorted and accounted for by fences. They had massive dirt paths of small crushed rocks that went on for a mile, and they had broken the river banks to nurture the lands with water. In the distance, they had seen something like Beaver's Tail constructions, but unlike anything that had ever been built. They radiated light and were visible for miles.

As they continued to march towards these constructions, they realized how massive they really were. One central structure went up for what appeared to be miles overhead, touching the clouds as they passed through its peak. And then they confirmed the sight of Eagle's Eye. Men with eagle wings were soaring overhead flocked as gulls around its towers.

The settlement itself was not grandiose, mainly composed of several longhouses and a central trading core, and their Beaver's Tails had been incredibly busy for the entire site had been surrounded by a large timber wall, and the tips of the timber had been filed to points. Only one entrance existed and it bustled with activity. As they drew nearer, they saw the walls were as white as the sandy beaches they had bordered, being reinforced with stone bricks.

Fearing the unknown, they kept their distance but it had been too late. Several of the flying men took notice and began their descent. The Deer's Horn trembled in fear as a squirrel awaiting the talon. Instead of that horrific, cold nail piercing into their chest, they landed before them gracefully and with open arms approached the Deer's Horn.

"Please, don't be afraid. We are your kinsmen." One of the angels announced.

"You... you have wings. How?" replied the Deer's Horn.

"I think you can tell. We are not from around here. You are in welcoming company. We're your new neighbours. Your brothers and sisters have befriended us and we now live alongside them."

"How long have you been here for?"

"Oh. About twenty years. The years have been good to us. Let me show you around."

The angel proceeded to walk the tribespeople through the land, and introducing them to their long lost kin. They traversed the avenues of the marketplace, always bustling with business. They even saw the newly built wharf with docked fishing ships. Eventually, their path led to the Temple of Lights, which had been embellished into a tall, ivory tower.

They stepped inside where the temple had been refined into a court hall and saw many dignitaries consulting with the locals. On all sides were many rooms where discussions were taking place. Down the center hall led to a great throne room.

Upon entering the throne room, they witnessed an archangel, much greater than any other angel they had seen yet. He had four wings, and sat on a large throne that had been cast from gold and upholstered in satins. The throne sat in front a golden gate, one which had clouds resting behind and filled the room with light.

One of the Deer's Horn stood in awe as he pointed out the gates to the rest of them.

"Oh, that?" said the king, "That's just heaven. Yeah, we come from there. I know, right?"

"Who are you? How do you speak the Spirit Tongue?"

"I think what you mean to say is 'Who are we?' Well, we're angels from the heavens. We've come to bring prosperity, order, truth and virtue to your land. Would you like to know more?"

"I have to say. I am intrigued. We are of the first tribe, and we are the Deer's Horn."

"Do you have a name? I am King Theocrites. And you are?"

"Names? What are names?"

"Name is what you call yourself. It is how we distinguish ourselves from our brothers. Say I said Deer's Horn. You and your brothers are bound to respond. Someone says Theocrites, well, that's me!" Theocrites then chuckles, "Don't worry, we'll fix that shortly."

"I'm sorry. Fix that? We are fine, thank you. We were always fine. It has been a pleasure to witness your culture, but we must be going."

"What? Leaving so soon? But you just got here."

"We must leave and return to our tribe. They are afraid."

"Oh. Well, so be it. You can tell them this. If any horrible circumstance befalls your people, we'll be right beside you. We're your neighbours now."

Theocrites then waved, and his guards escorted them out. On the way back to the road, they are handed the leashes of two large goats that have been saddled with large bags of seed.

The angel looked at him as he pointed to the goats and said, "This one is Katrina, and this one is Burt. Take good care of them. They are the finest milking goats in the neighbourhood. Well, Katrina is. Burt should help with the breeding."

"Thank you." The Deer's Horn responded as he accepted the gifts.

The Deer's Horn felt light weighted as they began their journey home. Their trip went by uneventfully, and every so often a shadow in the form of an angel skimmed over the plains.

Several of the Stalker's Fang were chosen to enter the swamps, for they know not what to expect. The Fangs waited for night when their night vision would benefit them. They slowly crept through the weeds of the treed border. Once they entered the swamp they slowly treaded their way through its dry outcroppings, avoiding water at all cost. They even favoured fallen limbs over the water. As they continued they made an effort to remember the safest and fastest way to return in case they needed to escape. In the distance they saw torchlight. They slowly made their way toward it.

Among the trees on a mound sat a small community around a bonfire. The bonfire had been muffled and kept the air warm with its coal. The people were in shambles, covered in mud, hair knotted and full of mange.

"We know you're out there. Show yourself, demon! Or is it you? That filthy cur of a herald they sent on their behalf." said one of their elders.

The Stalker's Fangs decided to approach the people.

"We are your kin." the lead Stalker's Fang announced, "What happened here?"

"We have no kin. You abandoned us. Now demons come for us. It's hopeless."

"What are these 'demons'?"

The elder looks up in a deep sorrow, "They are evil spirits. They have come from the belly of the world itself to devour us all. They have taken our strong and our beautiful. They only left the decrepit and the children behind. Now we are left here to rot."

"Now, now, that's just children's stories. Where are the rest of you?"

"I tell you the truth! See for yourself. Be careful though. There are demons in the swamps. Even on this very night. They smell your goodness and your love. Cake yourself in this soil. It will help."

The Stalker's Fang looked among each other and shrugged. They began to smear the perfuse soils against their clothing and their faces as they nearly gagged.

"In which direction can we find these 'demons'?"

"Head west until you hear the noises. You'll know what I mean when you hear it."

As they continued through the swamp, the Stalker's Fang deliberated on their escape. They decided that they would still remain on the path they had entered on. Even though it was longer than taking a direct path home, it was known to them and their assailant would have to travel the same distance if they were to chase them out.

They began to hear noises from below and fire light emanating from the ground. They crept closer to the source where they saw long, veiny lines of brick. They peered down the veins, and saw large beasts deep below them, clawing at the earth and tearing rocks from it. Many other beasts had been rolling small carts full of rocks glistening with ores. Larger beasts were whipping them with long strands of leather braided with nails. After receding, they took note of several other veins, and they all appeared to be converging not far away.

They began to follow the veins to the source. In the distance, they heard sounds of music and cheer. They were expecting vile sounds of horror, but the sounds were alluring. They continued to near the music and entered into a clearing. The clearing was very large. Every tree in its perimeter had been fallen and used to erect a gigantic keep with a great wall made of pitch and black stones. The entire clearing had been vacant and the noise was resonating from within.

The Stalker's Fang crept toward the main gate and it creaked open. They looked inside.

Humans and demons had been dancing among each other with a great feast laid before them. One massive beast was sitting on a large throne, dressed in plates of obsidian wreathed in fire and souls. It was unlike anything they have ever seen. It was as if the souls and fire were converging on his chest. The fire and souls were moving.

The demon called out to the people, who halted their dancing. After a short communication with the people, the demons began to feed on them and take them for their own. The humans responded and began taking demons.

The large demon rose from his throne and pointed towards the Stalkers Fang, roaring "Guards! Seize them!"

The Stalker's Fang quickly exited the clearing and began sprinting through the swamp, using their gift of travelling on fours to weave through its trees and fallen branches. The demons were quick and followed their tail, toppling weaker trees as they plowed through in pursuit. One of the demons managed to grab hold of a Stalker's Fang by the leg and had ripped it from its tree, slamming it to the ground. The demon began flaying its flesh.

The others began to hasten as adrenaline filled their veins. The demons were still on their tail but the openings to the plains were visible. The entire journey in the swamp had been amidst the darkness, but day was shining through the clearing as if it were midafternoon. They eventually escaped into the clearing where Horse's Manes were waiting with steeds. They make their escape as the demons reach the end of the swamps and stop in their tracks.

They returned to the council tribe in remorse, head hanging for leaving their kin behind, tears welling up in their eyes and washing the filth from their faces.

The council had been enjoying a mixture of fine milk and grains, celebrating the news of their new allies to the north. The celebration halted as the smell of death approached.

"Where is your brother?" The Stalker's Fang councilman called out.

"He fell to a ferocious beast. Our kin to the south called them demons."

"What is a demon?"

"They had unleashed the evil spirits from the belly of our world into the land. We saw it for ourselves. They had been scraping at its stomach, heaving rocks from its inner walls and building an effigy of darkness. They began celebrating with them and then, they began feeding on each other and partaking in each other's flesh. It was horrible. Their leader sent his minions to hunt us down. My brother was eaten by one in our escape."

The Stalker's Fang councilman rose and hugged the child, then began walking them toward their well.

"Here, let's get you cleaned off. Our gracious neighbours to the north had given us grain and milk unlike we have ever tasted. It will cheer you up. I promise."

The other Stalker's Fangs followed and began cleaning themselves off. One of their elder shamans from the Rabbit's Foot gave them paste made from milk thistle and lye to wash with, and began chanting songs of restoration upon them.

Their kin embraced them and fed them until they all drifted to sleep.

For a generation, our people continued within the plains but steered clear of the swamp's edge. During the night, the Stalker's Fang and Bear's Paw would patrol the south boundaries and had learned how to fell the beasts that would attempt to cross. Our gracious neighbours to the north continued to gift us and provide us with sustenance without cause. They even attempted to teach our gifted in their skills of refining the land. We would accept their gift, but we made it clear that our culture was our own.

In time, our people would begin to question the state of things. Will this ever end? A meeting took place between our elders where they would decide the fate of our people and our neighbours. Then something peculiar happened. A man, twisted with metals running through his body approached us. He had the most generous of smiles.

"Greetings neighbours!"

At first it startled them, and the guards took up their spears to keep its distance. The child Stalker's Fang, now a woman and leader of the Stalker's Fang responded.

"This is not one of their demons. Let him speak."

"Oh! So I see you have met the demons. Please, let me introduce myself. I am Michael, and herald of Mechanus. I am here to speak to your leader."

"I am Kytara of the Stalker's Fang. We are all leaders here. How did you find us?"

"My master sits at the top of the greatest peaks in the southeast. He monitors your land and he pointed me to you. My master wishes to speak to you. He bears great tidings for your people and wishes to aid you in this predicament. Will you accept his invitation?"

A deliberation began between the leaders, and the Deer's Horn rose.

"I will go. I am Stagart of the Deer's Horn. My tribe provides unity for our people, so it would be best for me to speak to your master."

"Wonderful! Please, follow me! You can tell me your story on the way."

On their journey into the mountains, Stagart began telling the Mechanoid of the break up between their peoples and the grace and tragedy that befell them a generation ago. He then continued into how it had changed their culture and his people were becoming upset.

"You have nothing to fear. What my master is about to propose will be of some benefit to you."

The Mechanoid then escorted Stagart to the tower and its crowning turret where the representative waited for him. The room itself was very large and filled with bookshelves. He sat behind a large cherry wood desk on what must have been the most comfortable looking chair of finely decorated wood and upholstered in loden green velvet.

"Ah! You must be Stagart of the 'Deer's Horn', as it were. I am the representative of Mechanus. I apologize for not introducing ourselves further, but your civilization at first was viewed on as primitive and indigenous. We had no idea how cultured your people have been until recently." said the representative.

"Well, thank you for taking notice, I guess..." said Stagart.

"Please, follow me. Our discussion will continue much easier if you witnessed current events."

The representative led him to a parapet door, where Stagart could have an encompassing view of the entire land. Although they were so high above the land, the air was so clear that they could see to the furthest reaches of the oceans and even the islands beyond.

"You know, it took me some time to acquire this device," he then tapped on a machine attached to the wall of the turret, "this thing generates an energy field that forces the air as still and dense as glass and even aids in the visibility of things far away. It is capable of assisting with your focus on objects at long distances. It is such a treat to have a world that lacks pollution."

Stagart replied, "Slow down. Start at glass again, or we can just call it your magic."

The representative then quickly corrected him, "Please don't resort to magic. Our people were hindered for over a thousand years because of simple judgements like that. If you heat sand to the point that it melts, it becomes clear and viscous, then rigid as it cools. We call it glass and make strong barriers with it that protect us from the elements and even flying objects, while providing us with vision that a wall could not. Energy is the source of life in all things, which we have learned to harness in purer forms, like the material the lightning that falls from the sky during a storm is made of. It is actually made of very small grains of sand, smaller than we can feel called 'electrons' which can travel within objects and even powers our bodies. We had learned to harness this energy in the most fabulous of ways."

Stagart was baffled, "Your wisdom amazes me. Compared to our culture, how far have you gone with this knowledge?"

The representative chuckled, "Well, take your culture; say several hundred years old before the angels and demons lived among you. Take all your experiences of all your people. Now think of where you were in the start, animals among animals, without even a sense for clothing. Think of where you are now. Think of all of the things you have ever had to do to grow as a people to now. Now take that time and effort, magnify it by billions of people over thousands of years."

Stagart shook his head and asked, "What is a billion?"

"Let's just put it this way. We have come from an unfathomable future to your people, but do not be afraid for we are here today to help you preserve your culture."

"Thank the spirits! They have brought you to us. Our people have been wondering if this will ever end. They just want their home."

"Unfortunately this will never end. These civilizations have claimed right to your land and your kin had accepted them in. They're mortal now and if a war would ensue it would devour them both. I think the angels like living, too. That could be a factor."

"So then what are you going to do?"

"You see that island over there? If your kin do not wish to live here anymore, ask among your people who do not wish to live here anymore and they can live there."

"That is not preserving our people."

"Look. You have to face it. This is your world now, and your old world is never coming back. Giving you that island is the best we can do for you. I promise you, it will remain untouched by the rest of the world. They will be able to continue on in their blissful preoccupations undisturbed."

"Well, considering the other options, we'll take it. So why did you have me come all this way?"

"So I can introduce you to the kings of the other nations. Look down there. They are nearly here."

"Those are the demons! They enslave and feed on our people! They breed with them and make abominations! Why do you bring them here?"

"Don't worry. They are forced into behaviour on our summit, and I have been informed that this particular demon has regrets and hopes for repentance. He should be docile enough."

As the other two leaders arrived, the representative met them at the doors and led them to the top of the tower where Stagart waited. He then continued on to explain the terrain as it existed that day, and the implications that would affect their rule.

After the discussion, they returned to the study where a feast had been prepared for them. They sat at a table and enjoyed pleasant conversation. Even the demon king had been lightened by the mood, but appeared to have a heavy heart. Each ruler then parted ways in the morning.

When Stagart returned, he called for a meeting of all the tribes. Wolf's Howls cross the plains gathered the people and a multitude formed outside their council's tent. He then explained the situation and the terms the representative has made for all people. At first, the people were confused and question this verdict and even his rule, but after explaining the absolute and unequivocal authority he had presented to them, they understood that there was no other way. They would have to choose. A period of woe covered the people as they divided once more and their families were torn apart by a need to leave the land. Those who wished to leave for Belliscia went to Elysica where boats awaited them.

The people began to question, "If all of this is true, how are we supposed to 'utterly destroy' our assailants? How can they claim that kind of power? Our brothers have been fighting the demons for a good while now and many of them have fallen at their hands."

Stagart responded, "I have no idea, but from what I have seen I would not doubt their ability."

At that moment, the ground began to tremble. Off in the distance a convoy of great steel wagons spewing smoke and soldiers leading came down from the mountainside. They made their way toward the gathering and circled it. A Mechanoid draped in fineries and ornate metals stepped forward.

"Hello, I am Colonel Marius. We are here to provide for you."

The sides of the wagons folded open and became ramps, and the Mechanoids began offloading supplies. The supplies were of the finest quality.

"Please, line up based on your tribes. We have significant tools for each of you to aid you in your development."

The Mechanoids began supplying the people with tools, clothes, tents, armour and even weapons. They were surprised because most of what they were given looked exactly like what they already use, but much newer.

"Don't look surprised," Marius said, "they may look similar but they are in fact made of space age materials. Even the armour is nearly impenetrable. Your tents will survive 200 years of the most brutal weather. It's easy to clean, too. There are plenty of consumable products here for your people to use. My people will teach you how to use them. If you start running low on supplies, just let us know."

They spent the afternoon showing the tribespeople how to properly use all the new gifts they had bestowed upon them, and then the convoy returned to the mountainside.

For a while, our tribe lived in peace. Every so often commotion could be heard from the swamps. Then, a war must have erupted, for the air itself was wreathed in fire in the night. Wailing onslaught could be heard for miles in the distance. Even then, demons never crossed into the plains for an age.

Then it happened. Demons began crawling out and into the plains. They were not vagrant demons. They were demons looking for more. They began actively hunting our people, even though they were under command to leave us alone. The Bear's Paws and Stalker's Fangs reciprocated. Their weapons were so great that they could fell a beast as if it were just a man. The blades were so sharp that they would sever limb from body. Their spears were capable of piercing the densest of armours.

For a while our people were naïve and enjoyed the gifts they had received. A queen among the angels offered assistance but our leaders refused. She had gifted them with a scroll from heaven, and they tucked it away. What happened next was our fault.

Fending them off was not a problem, but it was exhausting. The warriors never complained, but it became a full day's task to hunt the beasts down. Every so often, one would sneak through but they wouldn't survive long for the Eagle's Eyes became properly trained in bow and arrow, and even the arrows were plentiful and easy to find once they had been fired.

After a while, the demons began crossing over in desperation. Our weapons were beginning to blunt, our armour was falling apart. We were guaranteed 200 years of durability. I do not suspect Mechanus was capable of grasping the demons' persistence or resilience.

A group of Eagle's Eyes and Horse's Manes were asked to cross into Mechanus to ask for more provisions. One party was sent to the mines, the other to the representative's tower. After a week, they returned. The mines had been abandoned and only had mindless automatons digging for ores. The representative's tower had been vacated. There was no one left to answer the call. Even the portal to Mechanus was gone.

The demons began breaking our lines. One by one, our brothers began to fall. Demons began running loose among the wild grain, devouring our animals and hunting our tribe. Then the angels interfered. They began hunting the demons for us and helped us reclaim and heal our land. It was not enough. At first there were only vagrant demons that would run amuck, and the angels would hunt them down. It turned into full battles, with small armies facing off among the plains. Their battles would tear our land apart and left bodies of angels and demons in the dirt.

Our human neighbours began to cross our plains. There was something odd about them. They had the accent of demon and angel blood about them. Demons were crossing over into the angel kingdom, and angels were crossing into the demon kingdom. We did not know why, but we never questioned it. Their business was their own.

And now, here we are. Our land is scarred. We had given up repairing it, for every time we did it would continue to be sundered. We understood our fate, and rather than facing it, we lived around it, favouring the off beaten path and keeping to ourselves. Our proud tribe had become a tribe that lived in fear in its own home. Then Sorrownote and Syrenne came along.

Sorrownote of Wolf's Howl and Syrenne of Eagle's Eye gave us hope again. Their music helped us to flourish and gave us back our pride. Now we stand united, and the land is beginning to heal. They had also taught us the Elysican language, so we may ask the angels and the people of the north for assistance. We thanked them and honoured them for their presence among us. They will one day be the council members of their tribes. For now, they have chosen to continue to grow wise, and decided to enter Dornar where more had to be done.

*****

Journal Entry,

Although it was a satisfying experience to be loved and honoured by our people, it wasn't enough. Syrenne and I had decided that we must traverse the swamp and find the source if this cursed filth.

It was strange, the experiences that we had encountered. When we first set foot in the Dornarian Swamp we expected the worst. Demons feeding on demons, only the gross and most dominant of beasts remaining, but it was in fact much different. The swamps trembled in fear and its residents constantly looking over their shoulder, embracing the open hours of light for survival. For once the darkness came, so did instinct.

In the darkness, the calls of the malevolent erupted, and the cries of the fearful shrilled. In the darkness, it was feeding time.

There were few villages capable of holding their own in this backwater country. Those who did learned of their twisted fate and realized their ability to tempt it with goodness. The stronger communities became resistant to the beckoning of the reigning king and his army of abominations, but their blood constantly yearned for satisfaction.

We learned that our melodies could calm their blood and help them gain conscience. Our music would not only convey tragedy but bring hope. Our selfish spite against demons became hope for those regaining their humanity. So we continued to play, as we do today, feeding the spirits of those who appear to be so lost.

Then it came to us. They must not all be demons. Is it possible that the bloodlines crossed somewhere in the past? So we questioned the people. Lo and behold, not only were there humans being protected by these beasts, but the beasts themselves had been their kin born of demon blood. They were considered to be the first of the Dornarian Lineage, not borne of the fiery pits of hell or of this land but tied in between. Their birth was consequential and a product of coincidence. They had seen the human side in their kin and loved them as their own nonetheless. They had also been born with the capacity for good. Unfortunately they have a yearning and a calling given to them from their parents, so when the time comes they are forced to decide where they would live.

Very few Dornarians ever lived within the Capital City Dornar, for their blood was weak and they would fall victim to greater and darker powers. Most of the ones who choose exile live in the wilderness of the swamps, which is where the random calls of malevolence echo.

We also learned that the demons rarely left their city. Demons are too infatuated with vanity to enjoy the much simpler preoccupation of random hunting in the wilderness. Yet every once in a while, a demon with the right thirst will exit the walls and enjoy a pleasure diversion amongst the villages. It is on those nights that Syrenne and I feared for our lives.

The people had built a love for us, but the love was bitter to the demons. This displeased them and rather than hunting for pleasure they would rampage in hatred. There was something about love and serenity that disgusted them so. Even love among the Dornarians was forbidden to lessen the odds of an attack.

During our visits, we came across a woman named Moranda. She was a witch. Not a demon invoking practitioner of the black arts, mind you, but a sweet and gentle child of nature who embraced the natural energies of the land that came before the demons. She told us the history of Dornar.

Moranda was a dear woman who had aged very well among her people. She had isolated herself, maintaining her people's wisdom of the swamp land and the gifts it could provide. She also had knowledge of the spirits, far beyond even the Rabbit's Foot Tribe. She was capable of harnessing the spirits and focusing them as tools. She was even capable of manipulating the spirits into objects. One of her greatest objects happened to be her home.

She told me of her home once, and why it was never in the same place. Long ago, she came across a special gem that was perfectly round. It was even rounder than a pearl. She tempted the spirits to live inside of it to improve on its beauty, not knowing what it would hold in the future. Eventually she began to make her home with her kin, a simple Rabbit's Foot hut made of leathers and branches, with a cozy tree and a small fountain.

They began to enchant the land with the spirits, and the most mystical of plants began to bloom around the tree. The tree itself became lively. Its hues became more brilliant and the herbs and mushrooms would grow on its bark. They also enchanted the water, keeping it forever pure even with the darkest of taints. One could throw a handful of mud and dung into the water, and it would disappear in its crystal ripples. They built a meat locker within the hut, but the meat never perfused. The meat would also find preservation and would remain perfectly cooled without the need for a deep stone basement.

The swamp's sundering had begun. It started to turn into a bog under the death and coil caused by the demon's rank nature. They found their way to her hut and hunted her kin. Afraid for her fate, she hid among the trees, and held onto her marble, rubbing it for comfort. Her home then shrunk to the size of the marble and hid within it. It can still be seen within the marble to this day.

Upset with her fate, she tossed the marble away, as if to shun the very memory of her home. Instead of losing the marble, it had loosed her home into a clearing, and surrounded it with a hedge and moat. There was a little bridge welcoming her home. She went running inside to meet her kin, but they lay there dead. They hadn't aged a day. She began to weep over their bodies.

There was a clambering outside her home. In fear she screamed. The demons looked up and over the hedges, but it was as if they had not seen or heard her. They continued on their way. One began marching toward her home. It had stepped near the bridge that would let it in. Then, it disappeared. Moranda looked around, and it had appeared on the other side of her home. It was then that she realized that she was inside the marble, and the marble had grown her home back to normal size.

Then she realized why her family had not aged or decayed. She buried them properly, but began placing meats in the yard. She would call back the marble for a day, and laid it out again. It had perfectly preserved the meat as if time stood still within the marble.

Sitting in her tree, she began to dream of the perfect complement of herbs to chew on. Then she smelled them. The herbs were growing on the tree as she thought of them. She realized that the tree not only supported the life of the herbs she planted before, but it had managed to grow them on command.

From the moment we met Moranda, we knew that we would find sanctuary in her safe haven hut. When the demons would become violent, she was the first we would run to see.

Well, I believe I have told you enough. Now enjoy Moranda's story. Be careful, for the following content is very saddening and full of a culture built on the darkest of life paths.

*****

The Demonic Kingdom of Dornar

I, Moranda, have lived here for close to a century now. I don't look it, do I? Well, that is because I fare in blessing of my land, for I know it well and I know how I fit within it. It is such a shame what these people have become, so lost. They don't even realize how much they belong here and how that parasite-filled, gaping wound called Dornar had manipulated them into disaster.

I can tell you this. Darkness was never meant to be evil and malevolent like those things in the swamp. Darkness itself is as pure as light. It allows us to sleep and recuperate from a long day's work, it aids us in our gathering, and provides us with nutrition and remedies that the light cannot. It's just too bad that they were tossed into the darkness and not into a trash heap. I guess everything has its place for a reason. One day I hope to find out.

As I take it, Dornar was founded simply. A few bewildered travelers, aimlessly following the so-dubbed "Leader of Darkness" into the swamps. What they found next astonished them. There was nothing to fear. Not even the beasts prayed on them, for the beasts had their own tastes in flesh. The entire swamp lived and breathed for itself. Sure when they were a younger tribe they avoided it, but now they learned to embrace it.

The people of Dornar began building small villages out of fallen timbers which had been preserved by the swamp's waters. Outcroppings of land were more than stable, capable of supporting entire communities. The land was very fertile, having minerals and nutrients washed down from the mountains and trapped by the stagnant tides and low lands.

A blessing soon became idolatry. The people began worshipping the darkness as if it were their deity. By influence of their Leader, they claimed that the darkness itself had to be respected for providing them with such sustenance.

After a while and with great investment, the people poured their efforts into building a temple. They called it "The Temple of Darkness". Inside, acolytes would enter trance-like worship, beckoning to the darkness to provide them with more. It was as if the land just didn't provide enough. It was their first mistake. The acolytes grew more corrupt and fell into vice, believing that satisfying the darkness would in turn allow the darkness to satisfy them. Vice turned into malice, and they began sacrifice and vice against each other, in order to reflect the nature of the darkness.

Then, the swamp's stomach grumbled.

A hole in the floor before the altar crumbled, and nothing but shadowy fires and vapours of brimstone escaped. Then, they saw claws. Beasts of a demonic nature began to scramble out of the hole and surrounded it, hissing at the acolytes to keep their distance.

Four demons began clawing their way out with one hand and gripping chains over their backs with the other. As they exited the hole, they pulled out a massive throne, with a devil sitting upon it.

The devil announced "I am Solacrinus, and I am here to be your King. Worship me."

The Leader of Darkness stepped forward and claimed "This is my conjuring, and I have summoned you. The Darkness has brought you to me to serve me."

The devil leaned forward from his throne and sniffed at the Leader's neck, "Belladonna as a fragrance? Delicious." He then devoured his neck as his body dangled, head rolling onto the bare floor. As the body followed to the floor, Solacrinus reeled his head back and howled. He then faced his crowd and muttered, "What he should have considered is how he should prepare for when 'the Darkness' answers."

The devil then announced "I am Solacrinus and I am here to be your King. Worship me. I will make all of your darkest temptations come to fruition!"

And the acolytes began to worship Solacrinus. The acolytes would worship until they collapsed, starved and knees bleeding, only to be fed to the devil's lesser demons near him. As the acolytes began to die off, the devil turned to a survivor.

"You are stronger than the rest. The Darkness has chosen you, my child. Do my bidding and I will reward you greatly." grumbled Solacrinus.

The acolyte responded "With all my will, my liege."

"Gather more acolytes. The worship must persist."

So, the acolyte began going from town to town, pacing himself to ensure the incoming stream would replenish the acolyte population as they died. This process went on for five years. After five years, the people began to question this herald of the devil. After a while, Solacrinus invited the inhabitants of the swamps to witness his greatness.

The people gathered to Dornar, where they witnessed the ingenuity of their new guests. The demons had been summoning acolytes for worship and for slavery. The exhausted and malnourished were then either fed upon or cast into the pit, and the cycle of agony and labour never ended. They had been building long, narrow, winding veins of tar and stone, separating land from water and reaching far out into the distance. Within the trenches, demons and humans alike were being burdened with excavating giant fissures and dug deep into the earth, below the bog and into the rock beneath. They had been carving massive blocks and smelting ores. All of this was to build a keep, twisted and malformed, black as pitch and mortared with the subtle whispers of forsaken souls.

Solacrinus now exited the keep and stood before the people, shouting, "Welcome to Dornar Keep, the hub of all that is glorious in this land. I am your King! Solacrinus! I have prepared a worthy feast of rare delights for you and your kin."

His tone then changed into a pleasant beckon, "Come, imbibe in our provision and heed my call, for in your future there lies unsurmountable satisfaction."

Solacrinus stepped aside and bowed to the people, ushering them into the keep. The people, puzzled by this gesture, entered the keep.

The first doors led into an expansive courtyard, where cobblestone trails formed labyrinths of walkways in the trimmed sedges. The walls were as pitch as the exterior. They had been draped with long tapestries depicting horrific war scenes, often which showed the protagonists falling victim under the antagonists' might, scenes of brutality and malice, all of which resembled the inspirations of their host.

Long tables and benches had been laid out, made from the wood of the toppled forests, hand carved by claw and sheer force, grated down into an upsetting yet impressive feat of craftsmanship.

Minstrels lined the walls, Incubi and Succubae enchanting their audience with instruments and sounds never heard before. The music became entrancing, relaxing their audience who then began to imbibe voraciously on the feast laid before them.

All sorts of wildlife and swamp legumes had been prepared in a manner never tasted before, and the ales and wines. There was something about the ales and wines that enflamed their blood and their hearts.

Entranced by the music and filled on unique pleasures, the people began to dance. Demons began to move within the crowd and dance among them.

At that moment, the main keep doors opened and King Solacrinus was being carried out on his throne by demons.

"My people: As your king, I have a charge for you. There are only two positions within my land: the worshippers, and the worshipped. Which will you be?"

The people looked at each other confused and continued to dance.

Demons began taking hold of those in the crowd, and either feeding upon them or taking them for pleasure.

"You may be worshippers, or the worshipped. There is no other room under my reign. Which will you be?"

One man shouts out, "The Worshipped!"

Solacrinus points to the man and declares, "Then take your prize!"

Solacrinus let out a trembling guffaw as he witnessed the man taking hold of a succubus. The crowd, intoxicated by poisoned delights, began to turn on each other, and what happened next birthed a new generation of Dornarians.

Amidst the wickedness, the front doors had creaked open and shadows were visible, peering through its cracks.

"Guards! Seize them!" Solacrinus howled.

Several of his elites burst out of the doors and began chasing down their witnesses.

The Dornarians became the greatest beasts of burden. Strong with demon blood yet docile with human blood, they never showed an ounce of rebellion and slaved until the bitter end. It was not long until the core of Dornar had been built, massive and winding buildings, crumbling under their own expanse, then reinforced with bracing lumber and stone. Many bridges had been built over the fissures. Slaving Dornarians can be witnessed from the surface to this day.

After 20 years, Solacrinus was getting old. He could not understand why. His form was becoming decrepit as the humans do and yet he was an immortal spawn of hell. Since he began his reign, he had never left his keep. Not even to visit the rest of the developing core. His entire stay had been lived in luxury and vanity, never having to leave his throne room.

Solacrinus then called for a scout to traverse the land and seek an answer to his riddle.

The scout never returned.

Solacrinus called for a scouting party to traverse the land. The party never returned.

Solacrinus then called for one of his champions, Baalthezar, and his mighty warriors to locate the bodies of his slain scouts and deliver an explanation.

Baalthezar was the first to cross the Blood Plains and witness the great fields of Elysica. The aromas of grain pollens filling the air was upsetting to them, bringing with them temptations for the scent of death and agonizing pain. Then, in the distance, he saw them. Angels were flying overhead, like a flock of songbirds over what must have been a temple with a tall, ivory tower which rose toward heaven.

"Not here," Baalthezar muttered, "This land had been given to us. It is our privilege. They must be ended. Their kind has no place in our world."

At that moment, an angel had been seen casually floating overhead and locked eyes with Baalthezar. She then buffeted into the sky and soared toward the temple.

"Catch her! She must be stopped!"

Two of Baalthezar's minions took flight after her as Baalthezar and the other minions sprinted on all fours. A high pitched call filled the air and a multitude of angels gathered to ensnare the demons. It is not long before Baalthezar and his minions had been taken prisoner.

In a large, mangled net, they are dragged toward Elysica Keep. They were dropped at the doorstep, where they were halted by guards donning white jade plate armor trimmed in silver and ivory, wielding broadswords of great refines and tower shields bearing heraldry of the heavens.

As the massive limestone and cedar doors opened, a king among angels stepped forward.

"So it's true. I thought I recognized you, Baalthezar. One never forgets a traitor."

"Hello, Theocrites, it's good to see you again. I see you're growing feeble. So it isn't just us."

"And who is this 'us' you speak of? How many more are you?"

"You do not get out much. Still have your eyes focused solely on the heavens. It's a pity, you know. Our kingdom is so much greater than yours. We will feed on your flesh soon enough."

Theocrites shudders, "How I despise speaking to demons. Always makes my spine quiver. I'll tell you what, demon. I will show mercy on you and your ilk under one condition. You tell your master that I wish to meet him in the center of the Blood Plains. He may bring no more than four with him. If he does not, we will execute your colony end mass. Is this understood?"

"And if I do not?"

"I promise a quick and painless death."

"Then let us free."

With a simple gesture, the demons were surrounded by two dozen of king's high guard, and then released from their nets. Baalthezar and his minions dusted themselves off, hissed at the guards and the king, and made their exit. They were followed by the high guard on their journey home until they reached the edge of the swamps.

Baalthezar made his way back to the keep. On his way he would unleash his bitterness upon beasts in his way, tearing them apart with his bare hands. He arrived at the keep and was ushered in with haste. He and his minions now stood before Solacrinus.

"Baalthezar, so you are not dead after all." Solacrinus chuckled to himself, "Tell me. What has become of us? What have you seen?"

"I saw angels, my lord. The angels are here. And they too are colonizing. They are being led by Theocrites."

"ANGELS?!? And you did not bring their heads back for me? Instead you make us appear weak before them. You are lucky that I value your service Baalthezar," Solacrinus then peered at the minions, "Your minions? Not so much. To the pit with them!"

Solacrinus' elites emerged from the alcoves that border the room and rushed toward the minions. The minions clawed and grappled with the elites, but eventually were dragged and thrown into the pit and to the abyss. The elites then receded to their alcoves.

"So, Baalthezar, you managed to speak to the angels and Theocrites no less. Do tell. Why did he let you live?"

"He showed mercy my lord, so that I may deliver his demands."

"Demands? Yes, of course he would have demands. He already is aware of his frailties, I presume. Please, continue."

"He demands that you present yourself with only four of your soldiers. He claims he may have a solution. He also claims if you do not abide by his terms he will execute the lot of us."

"Oh, Theocrites. Still high and mighty. He will never learn how weak he really is. Perhaps this is the opportunity to show him. So be it. I will bring my elites. Baalthezar, please keep my throne warm for me."

"As you command, my lord."

Solacrinus then rose from his throne and began making his way toward the doors. Behind him, his four largest elites who donned plates of obsidian and trimmed with wrought iron, bearing sadistic axes and hammers with flaying edges. They assembled and filed two by two.

For the first time in years, Solacrinus set foot outside his keep, and bore witness to the core Dornar had built. It appeared that his demon kin had decided to elevate themselves in much grander temples, painted with their banners and heraldry, claiming power over Dornar.

Solacrinus turned his head toward his elites, "When we get back, first we will continue to build the keep. Then we will destroy these effigies of lesser demons."

The elites offered not so much as a flinch in response.

As Solacrinus and his elites began to cross the swamps, the beasts evaded their presence as if their foul stench had warned them of the oncoming onslaught.

As they crossed into the Blood Plains, banners were visible in the distance, sailing in the winds, luminescent with the sun's brilliant rays. Angels soared overhead, keeping a watchful eye on the edge of the swamp.

"Where are my banners? Did you bring banners?"

His elites raised up their weapons over their shoulders.

They made their way toward the banners. Theocrites stood at the foot of the banners, backed by two dozen of his high guards.

"You say bring four and yet you bring twenty four. Not a fan of fairness, are you Theocrites? How unangelic of you."

"This is not about fairness, Solacrinus. You and I know perfectly well that you would take any opportunity to end my life. We are here on even terms. Now we must journey together for two days."

"You still emit the light of the heavens. It disgusts me. At least with your age it appears dim and bearable for now. I will let it continue. So, where is our destination?"

"Apparently those who live among us and those who live among you were kin, and they had kin that traveled into the mountains. I suspect that they may have a solution. From what I've been told, the kin in the mountains had been more logical in their deliberations and may have the aptitude to understand the situation."

Solacrinus led the way without announcement. Unimpressed by his action but understanding of his attitudes, Theocrites allowed him to take the moment and followed.

Their path went unimpeded into the mountains and to the doorstep of a mine. What they saw then impressed them.

The gates to the mine were teeming with people and Mechanoids alike, bustling with activity among the shops and coffee houses. The entrance to the mine appeared to be guarded by larger Mechanoids, but unlike the others they were completely mechanized and armoured from head to toe. They also carried strange weapons, long sticks of steel with unwieldy handles. At least the tips of their weapons had blades mounted on them.

As the angels and demons stepped forward, the crowd grew silent. An old man in his last years stepped out from the cave and yet he seemed to have the vigor of a youth. He approached Theocrites and Solacrinus.

As he began his approach, he eyed Solacrinus, "Nope, nope, not to you..." and steered his path toward Theocrites.

The wise man then claimed, "Well look at you all. I guess my brothers were right. And here I was, trying to prove you all wrong. Wow. Angels and demons, huh? I'm surprised you're all so old... and feeble..."

Theocrites responded, "I don't know how to explain this, but we are dying. We don't die. We live forever. Can you explain what is happening to us?"

"Well, I can't, but I'm sure someone around here is. Do you see that? I was trying to disprove your existence. This thing wasn't even supposed to work. Out of a sudden, it opens on its own. I couldn't believe my eyes, then these things began pouring out and altering the world. One of them explained to me that they were just blood cells of the greatest organism of all time named "Mechanus" and they are seeking its soul. They didn't really give me an option of refusal, but who cares. Have you ever tasted coffee? They even installed a coffee maker directly into the portal."

Solacrinus burst out, "We know about this world, we know about all worlds. What is happening to us?"

The wise man, clearly unamused turned to the devil. "Wow. My first moment of glory and it's all 'me, me, me. Fine. Give me a second."

At that moment, he turns to what appeared to be a high ranking official of the Mechanoid community and requests "Fetch me a solution."

The Mechanoid then steps through the portal, and a crystal on the back of its head shimmered. Within moments, a helicopter carrier landed at the portal, and a representative stepped through into their plane.

The representative answered, "I will aid you, but the circumstances of your fates may span generations. If I do, you must promise me this: I will rule your land for all time. Not as a functioning body of government, but to maintain a balance that would keep you from destroying yourselves."

The leaders agreed to his demands, at which point he explained, "You are from immortal planes. Being immortal and without time was one of the governing mechanics of where you are from. We have been witnessing, here and in other planes, life crossing between planes adapts and conforms to the mechanics of the destination. That being said, now that you live in a mortal plane where death and decay is a natural occurrence and a mechanic of this universe, you are all now mortal. Not just mortal as in you may die, but you are also decaying on a cellular level, aging, and eventually you will die."

Solacrinus, displeased with his agreement yet understanding its clause, walked away unannounced with his elites following closely behind him.

The very discussion made Solacrinus aware of his predicament. How could a demon be aging? And with all those years of debauchery and solace, his choices began to take a toll on his body, making a stronger impression on him than his lost youthfulness.

The two day journey down the mountains, across the plains and back into the swamplands were exhausting. Solacrinus had not endured such an adventure in his entire stay, and now his bones could barely take the toll. A sigh of relief exited his maw as he approached Dornar.

Only days had passed since the excursion and Dornar had already begun to shift. The banners on the buildings had now reflected Baalthezar's sigil. Completely unamused, Solacrinus stormed into his keep with his elites following and saw Baalthezar sitting on his throne.

"I see you had become comfortable in my stead," Solacrinus said, "you must be mad to think you could overthrow my rule, sitting on my chair no less."

"Your rule?" Baalthezar responded, "I had been slaving in the quarries since I arrived. I had witnessed all the follies that had fallen upon us. 'Oh, no! I'm aging!' Whimpering like a school girl passing her prime years. If you hadn't holed yourself within these chambers you may have gained a dose of wisdom. Now look at you. Old and feeble. I am barely approaching my prime years!"

"Insolence! Guards! Seize Baalthezar!"

Not a single soldier made a motion.

"Even your people understand your wickedness. I have given them so much more to live for! The freshest meats. The finest concubines. The rarest treats. Their own kingdoms! Today begins the age of Baalthezar! Feast my children, and bring me his shell!"

In his last moment, Solacrinus muttered, "You are a fool, Baalthezar, and they will take you for one until the end of your days."

Then, demons swarmed Solacrinus and his elites, feeding on their flesh and ripping away his armor, which Baalthezar proceeded to mount over his own. The Rule of Solacrinus had ended, and from that moment, the Rule of Baalthezar began.

Unfortunately for Baalthezar, Solacrinus' final words carried a hint of truth. For every token Baalthezar gave his people, his people demanded more. The chaos of Dornar, free from persecution of rule, grew decadent. The streets became filled with vice, and the residents began to conflict with each other for personal gain.

Baalthezar's only strength was hiding his weakness. He feared his right on the throne. Like Solacrinus, he rarely ventured into the city.

It was under his reign that the demons began exiting the city, looking for villages and wild creatures to feast upon, and taking the villagers for their own. The balance of the swamp began to shift, and the swamp began to reflect the death it began to inhabit. Dornar itself had lost its central core, for the core was rotting amidst the greatness that surrounded it. The populace began springing up great towers, greater than the ones before, towers that would rise to the sky and honour their lords.

Lords came fresh from the abyss and met Baalthezar unchallenged. Baalthezar, hiding under his layers of armour was growing feeble in his age too, and it was only a matter of time they would also come for his flesh.

Armies were being forged in the names of the demon lords, who had heard of angels residing in the land. They wished to continue a war that began eons ago, when they were cast from the heavens into the depths of the abyss, the furthest corner from the light. They wanted revenge, and they would have it in the form of angel flesh.

The demons had learned that the pain and torment had been feeding them and making them strong. Unfortunately for those who died, they rarely found their way back for the depths of the abyss were vast and very few even knew of the portal's existence. Over time, as the armies grew, they became envious of each other's powers. Instead of preparing for war against the angels they began to war against each other.

During this time, a Mechanoid had found its way through Dornar and into his throne room.

"You must come with me! My lord demands it!" said the Mechanoid.

Baalthezar responded, "And what are you supposed to be? You are not a demon. This is obvious."

"I am from Mechanus, and we have great news to share with you. The audience of the angel king and yourself had been requested once more. Please, hurry!"

The Mechanoid then approached the throne and pulled at his hand, attempting to pull him from his throne.

"Are you not afraid, strange one?"

"Afraid of you? You look like a teddy bear... with lots of plates and a big gaping maw mind you."

"This may benefit me." Baalthezar then announced, "I must travel into the mountains to amass even greater treasures! This simpleton wishes to worship us with its fineries, precious metals and gems! I will return."

His audience chuckled as they continued on with their debauchery.

As they travelled toward the mountains, their conversation continued.

Baalthezar breaks the silence, "You mentioned that my audience had been requested once more. Are you speaking of Solacrinus? You must be confused. I am Solacrinus' heir."

"Heir? But Solacrinus was barely breaking into a mature age."

"Well, I may have overthrown his rule. As I look back, it was probably the first of many mistakes during my rule."

"For a demon you sound rather repentant."

"Being mortal does make one think. Could I have been a better king? Could this have been an opportunity for repentance? I have no idea what a demon is privileged to, but over time I like to think that I may have been accepted. I dream of being an angel again sometimes."

"Wait, wait, wait. You were an angel?"

"We all were. Well, most of us were. Many of us are fallen humans who chose a path of complete and utter disregard for ourselves and for those around us, falling into eternal damnation for the most mortal of sins, but yes. We were once angels.

"Eons ago, when time became time, our creator lived in absolute void. He created the light to be a source of life and in its purest concentration became a plane of its own. From this plane, he would then create other planes of existence. There was no great difference beyond this plane than the others, excepting immortality. Life itself can live on to eternity, and so could anything made from it. So, our creator decided to make beings from the light itself, and called them angels.

"Angels were the first of his living creations. Immensely powerful, he bestowed upon them the gift to travel to other planes in presence, in order to influence them without the need to live among them. Angels, being ever grateful for the gifts, lived a completely subservient life to the will of their creator.

"But there was one angel who did not like the life of servitude. He believed that with these gifts and blessing, why would they be limited to the whims of one mind. He began tempting the other angels and building a rioting mutiny. One fateful day, a riot took place in the heavens that divided brother from brother.

"Rather than spectating this war, our creator washed his hands of the situation and cast the rebels to the furthest corner of all the dimensions, into the darkness, the abyss.

"In the abyss we coiled in agony, starved of light and syphoned of power. After a while, the pain subsided. We remained present, and yet all the pain of life had left our bodies. We then felt a new presence. The darkness had begun soaking into our beings, filling us and twisting us. It gave us immense power and strength.

"Still concerned with the rebellion and ever hateful of heaven, our leader continued to stir our hatreds and began feeding on everything vile and reciprocal to the heavens they once knew. It was not until then the darkness became a living hell.

"For eons we waited. We watched the planes, tempted fates, even manipulated the populations of our creator's new favoured creations. His favourite was to accuse them and plant accusation into their hearts, convincing them into persisting with their faults and failure, leading them into ongoing destruction without escape. Then it happened. We discovered a worshipping congregation so enthralled by their belief that it had created a portal to cross over to the other side.

"Although we were mortal, we embraced the living air. The experience of a mortal plane is unlike any other. I have to say. We relished in its magnificence. So much so that we made a pact with each other, whether we stay or return to the pit on day, we would never divulge our secret. Hell must not know of this land, or it would consume it all."

The Mechanoid, enthralled by the story interrupts, "But what about your leader, the deceiver? Why hadn't he taken interest in our world directly? How can it stay such a secret?"

"He has his intentions fixated on a world with billions, and he's winning. Evil delights in victory. A world of mere thousands, even hundreds of thousands is dwarf in comparison. I doubt he'd care if he found out."

"So you are angels then?"

"We were once angels. We have been divided from our people for all eternity. Even if we die again, repentant or not, salvation is a gift only bestowed upon humans. This favour only adds to our jealousy of the mortals."

Through their conversation, the atmosphere of fear and wonder subsided between the two.

Baalthezar then asked, "As for you? What plane do you hail from? I have never seen technology like the kind you happen to be wearing."

The Mechanoid replies, "Good question. We were a simple world once, but two thousand years ago we reached the precipice of our own destruction. Our greed had destroyed our planet, and it was nearing collapse. Some of our greatest minds developed a form of computer that would be able to house the most articulate and advanced computer scripting in history. It was so advanced, that it would eventually begin to upgrade itself. Our scientists managed to create the first artificial intelligence.

"Over time, the intelligence was studied. We found that it was remorseless, incapable of weighting its decisions with empathy or even calculating alternate options. So, rather than giving it power, we spent two decades teaching it and feeding it knowledge of human history, its disasters, and its more fruitful ambitions.

"We then accepted its abilities and let it loose in our mainframes. Over time it began making factories capable of making robots. Robots were making robots, and the world eventually was covered by technology.

"At first it disgusted us. It plowed over entire forests and mountain ranges, but then it occurred to us why it made those decisions. It happened to be refining and recycling the resources into an absolutely efficient system. It was so efficient, that it became even greater than a sustained natural ecosystem.

"Through all its endeavours, there was still one prevalent thought in the system. It had envy for life and the living. It had spent 5 centuries destroying it, not embracing what it was destroying. Not only did it now live to serve life, but it wished to find a life of its own.

"The first five hundred years were difficult, but eventually the natural world became forgotten. Two thousand years later, we are now crossing dimensions on its behalf, seeking its soul. We don't really mind. For me it's a wonderful experience to witness other cultures in bloom."

Baalthezar smiled for the first time, "That is an incredible story. Perhaps I will see your kingdom one day."

The Mechanoid smiled in return.

Climbing through the mountains, Baalthezar and the Mechanoid finally reached a mountain top, where a great tower had been perched. They have been met at its doors by Theocritus and several high guards, along with the representative standing within its frame.

"Baalthezar?" Theocritus welcomes smugly, "So, I guess Solacrinus' reign came to an end. How does it feel to be in charge of hell?"

Baalthezar answers, "Well, it's hell. There's nothing like the air up here, that's for sure."

Theocritus then states, "At least you get a taste of what is good in this world before you return to your cesspool. An unfortunate series of events, the abyss must have been. Perhaps this is our creator's saving grace on your life. I hope it won't be as short lived as Solacrinus' life was."

Baalthezar lowered his head, reminded of his ambush that led to Solacrinus' life being ended. "I am a much better king."

"I believe it."

The representative, waiting patiently, pipes up, "Oh, I'm sorry. Am I interrupting? Oh, yes! To the matters at hand!" It was then the representative led them to the top of his towers, revealed the land and the islands to them and explained current events.

The representative then set out a great meal for them to partake in. They all sat around the table and discussed what they have learned. After the evening was over, Baalthezar began to walk home, completely despising the thought of returning to his kin.

For the next few years, Baalthezar lived mute and inattentive to his rule. The days drifted by as he dreamed of living among mortals, travelling to a vast plane of technological wonder, and envied a life free of this ridiculous perpetuation of sin and vice. Eventually, Baalthezar had been torn from his throne, his armour set asunder and thrown to all the corners of Dornar. Baalthezar was then remembered as "Baalthezar the Coward", for he hid in his armour, stature and resource to the day he died. Unfortunately, the secrets of his discussions died with him, and his people knew not of the fate of tampering with the Blood Plains or even war would have upon their people and the entire population of Draemoria.

It was only in time that Dornar would fall without leadership. In Baalthezar's rule, the population became demanding of their spoils and had erected their own towers in their name. The core had become a shade amidst many towers and keeps, nine in all. Each keep claimed the right to rule the land, for they had the greatest of the armies. The armies turned on each other and the Dornarian Civil War began.

The Dornarian Civil War carried on for three decades. The war was rampant and carnage filled the streets. Dornar would quickly reflect the abyss, becoming an endless chain of malice and iniquity. Demons continued to pour out of the pit, fueling the fire. Knowledge of the mortal coil had become privy information. The locals who knew would use it to their benefit, luring the newer demons into the city where they would become vulnerable to their sick and twisted desires.

Dornar became a hollow shell of its former glory. Its infrastructure lay war torn in the rubble, entire buildings had been toppled. Those buildings that had survived were sought after for shelter, in turn fueling the violence. Even the demons from the pit below disregarded the wonder of the mortal world. The population dwindled and the streets slowly became vacant. After the dust had settled, only the strongest of demons remained. These malevolent megalomaniacs bred into existence a new era of Dornar, one that would be stronger than ever.

For an age Dornar became a republic. Its leaders, wise from the three decades of destruction, set forth major guidelines that would allow the city to continue to flourish. Rules had never worked for demons before. Now that they understood their mortality, a level of conscience set in and the demons realized the purpose of the guidelines. Dornar continued on with its wanton satisfactions and thrived off parasitic chaos.

Even with the guidelines in place the swamps continued to rot and became bogs. After all of the violence and destruction the swamp had lost its balance and was no longer capable of sustaining life as it once did. There were still human villages but many of them became polluted with Dornarian blood. Even the creatures either adapted to their new environment or were too strong for the demons who wished to feed on them. The demons eventually forgot the taste of human flesh and the flesh of beast, and forgot about the human race entirely.

The core of Dornar retained its nine capitals that would each hold representation within the republic. The central temple where the pit existed then became a historical location and preserved in its condition. The nine leaders of the nine capitals surrounding the central temple each had a smaller throne that circled the pit, and each represented a cast of the circles of hell. Dornar embellished 'prime stock' lords from the pit. In memory of Baalthezar the Coward, the rulers were refused the right to bear armor and weapons. With their flesh exposed for its strength and eventually its weakness, great demons would eventually dismiss their command and throw them off their seats. The thrones themselves became a vile perpetuation of strength and wickedness.

As stated, the land had been broken into nine major segments that were governed to reflect the circles of hell. It was believed that in this segregation the chaos could be contained and in turn the kingdom would be given the opportunity to recover. Also, by taking on a form its residents could recognize they were less overwhelmed by occupying a mortal realm. They also felt free to travel between the circles, which was contradictory to the pit since the pit had been designed to punish the demons and the forsaken souls in a manner that was unsavoury to them. By opening the circles they could then find pleasure and enjoy the mortal realm as long as they would survive its atrocities.

The major segments would then take on form within the infrastructure and began repairing and twisting its architecture. The locations of each of these segments were expressed as hours on a clock, from one to nine, one being the most northerly segment.

At one o'clock, Limbo was the most peaceful of all the segments, had been left asunder and allowing the underlying foliage to overgrow and weave through the cracks in the roads and fallen buildings. Most of the Dornarian population found this land to be a land of rest for its occupants lived in a melancholy state, drifting in sloth and lacked any sort of ambition or drive. Wickedness could still be found in its corners as demons found Limbo to be stocked with 'easy prey'. Limbo had been set between heresy and fraud for it to preserve its calm and peaceful state, well, to the best of its ability.

At two o'clock, Heresy became the focal point of all sacrilegious ideals. The purpose of heresy was to feed lies to the masses, perpetuating false ideals and motivations that would stimulate the demons in their revitalization. The land had been covered in temples reflecting different aspects of belief systems and cultures, and confused the land as much as it had stimulated it. Neighbouring Limbo and Violence gave it the opportunity to thrive off violence and find solitude for meditation.

At three o'clock, Violence had set its foundation. Being one of the most savaged portions of Dornar during the civil war, its sundered infrastructure would be reinforced and improved upon to excite those with passion for war and violence. The fallen would then be exported to gluttony, to allow those who preferred demon flesh to enjoy its fruits. When conflict arose between demons, they would be forced to violence to contain the conflict and prevent a future civil war from brewing. Violence was set between anger and heresy, for they were the two greatest perpetuators of violence in all history.

At four o'clock, Anger became the fuel source for Dornar's passion. Violence would regularly erupt as demons would vent their frustrations on the world around them. Anger had been filled with distilleries and apothecaries, where their poisons would enflame the heart and propel their motivations. Those who indulged in anger preferred to vent among violence and lust.

At five o'clock, Lust had turned its buildings into hotels, taverns and brothels and the streets became riddled with fleshly amusement. The moon rarely set on lust for lust never slept. It had been given a segment directly across from limbo, for if they were neighbours war would be inevitable. It was found that anger and greed would be its best suited neighbours.

At six o'clock, Greed became the source of all material things, and converted its city scape into an industrial sector, complete with forges and smithies where all sorts of equipment and materials for structure had been provided. Greed had been open to the general population to provide all that was needed to rebuild Dornar, but the turnover in trade was criminal and next to slavery. Those who entered Greed on behalf of their people rarely returned. Greed had also built its infrastructure deep into the veins below Dornar to continue its mining occupation. Those who invested their lives in greed would mostly crave two things in life, being gluttony and lust.

At seven o'clock, Gluttony converted its land into farms and slaughterhouses, where they began domesticating creatures and demons alike. Only true gluttons would embrace living in this land, for it was perfuse with death and defecation. Very rarely would any Dornarian wish to stay in Gluttony longer than acquiring their goods, although Gluttony also had the best restaurants in the land and were very difficult to resist. Gluttony was found to be the most foul but necessary segment in the mortal realm, so neighbouring greed made it possible to adequately feed the labourers and neighbouring treachery would serve as a stench buffer for nobody cared what treachery would have to deal with.

At eight o'clock, Treachery became the prison for the most derelict of inhabitants. It had come to a point where some demons were just found to be too sick and twisted, reflecting hell itself and not accepting the stability the Dornarians had set forth for the mortal land. These demons would be cast into the prison where they would be whipped into submission. They also would become Dornar's greatest army for they were the mightiest and most relentless of all the demons. The residents were so afraid of these demons escaping that the entire segment had been capped to prevent escape. It is fabled that one day, when war would arise, the king would unleash this army on the world who would then decimate its enemies and sire a new world for demons among men. Neighbouring gluttony made the stench of death bearable for the rest of the segments and neighbouring fraud would provide a sense of fear for the new occupants.

At nine o'clock, Fraud had become an educational hub, where the people would be fed lies of what they could become within Dornar. Those who crawled out of the pit with no sense of direction or wisdom about them were sent directly to fraud where they were initially taught of the mortal world and what they believed they would need to know to traverse the other segments. In fact, they had been lied to, deceived with grandiose claims of invincibility and dominance, and then would fall under its boot. Fraud neighboured treachery and limbo, to provide fear and meditation.

After a time, the demon lords had gates built over the pit to prevent unwanted flow during times of rest for even the lords needed to recede to their castles and enjoy their vanities from time to time. Eventually the comforts of their domains became more tempting than ruling over the pit, so special days of celebration were called when the pit would be opened to unleash fresh blood into the land. The residents would then prepare for the influx, to steer those who began to pour out.

Word of the portal grew in the abyss and every demon who had been informed of its presence had to have their piece. The demon lords used this ploy to their advantage. Demons began to line up for the opportunity to pour out of the pit, but were not aware of the mortality they would encounter. Fresh demons became just as likely to become food as they were to thrive. The ones who did thrive were given the right to thrive. Their quality had been sought after for the blood of future generations. Very few ever wished to return to the pit and those who did were nourishment for their voice could not be trusted in the depths below.

It is believed that the republic carried on for a half of a century. It was the longest lived of all the reigns within Dornar. But, if one considered the amount of lords that had been cycled in the process, no single rule lasted for more than four years. Even the limbo segment had repeated changes in lineage for their leaders were weak willed.

It was then a new herald from the abyss came forth. His name was Gregarion. Gregarion had tact among the other demons that had never been witnessed before. It is believed that Gregarion sat near the portal for an entire century, watching from below and listening intently. When he emerged from the pit, he quickly vacated the keep in search of refuge without direction. He used his tact to manipulate the people, receding in conflict and becoming one with the darkness, cloaking his true ambitions as he made his way toward the lords. As he learned more of the mortal world, he armed himself with poisons and weapons that would deliver a swift death.

He then found his way to the lords. One by one he poisoned and fell them. One by one his competition fell away. It was then that he found the oldest of the lords were still living as putrid soothsayers in the fissures below Dornar.

Gregarion spent a decade under the guidance of these lords, recognizing them for their wisdom and gaining strength from mining the tunnels. In his spare time he relished in the stories of Solacrinus' reign and became obsessed with reclaiming his armour.

Gregarion realized that it was time to emerge from the depths and reclaim the throne. Since he had ended the lives of all the residing lords, the streets were filled with anarchy once again as the demons fought over the right to rule. In the confusion Gregarion tracked down the pieces of Solacrinus' armour and reassembled the suit. With his knowledge of weapons and mortality, he modified the suit to bear spikes and edges that would be soaked in poisons. Any man or demon who would challenge him would fall dead from a single prick.

Gregarion entered the throne room which had become a feeding pit, and approached the throne. He scraped away the cobwebs and dusted the seat. Gregarion then sat on his throne. Dornar had become a monarchy once more.

Gregarion's first command on the throne was to rebuild the working class. He began summoning demons that had a complement great strength and shallow will. With a new army of labourers, he would flush out all the decadent who in turn became food. The new labourers began amassing resource from the depths. The keep was then rebuilt and became the greatest structure of them all, toppling entire blocks of towers which spilled life of riots into the streets. Those who rebelled were slain on sight. Those who accepted their fate were inducted into his army. He then instructed his minions to gather humans so that he may gain control of Dornarian offspring. Very few villages remained, so only the choicest of human blood would be taken. The rest of them were forced into debauchery and the village population slowly began to flourish.

Gregarion began to be worshipped after all these great feats. He was considered the saviour of Dornar and elevated to godhood among men. He was the first king in the history of Dornar to openly walk the streets. It was then that he realized ruling wasn't gained by satisfying their desires for sin, but to invest in those desires that would bring productivity into their lives. To amass resource and population, this had brought satisfaction and sustenance. The population then forgot the taste of beast flesh. The villagers would breed as livestock.

With this new perspective on ruling, Gregarion would still achieve more than any other. Gregarion was the first demon king to sire children and live to the end of his days. He had fifty children in all, and they all desired a piece of Dornar for themselves. Gregarion had no rightful heir. He wished to utilize their ambition and lust for power to propel their strengths as they pitted against each other for rule. Each of his children had different mothers and was given different traits that would allow them to excel. They also began to build their own kingdoms and segregated Dornar into casts based on skills, abilities, and traits.

Dornar had become a republic again, but only for a time. The children had the pit sealed off by planks and boulders that overlaid the republic's gates. In the next 50 years, Dornar took its time away from grandeur. Gregarion's children realized Dornar was not ready for a new king, and that they were all equal in one way, shape or form. They would instead invest in their people directly. They began harnessing and evolving their strengths and learning to function as a whole. Dornar began to grow exponentially.

Even amidst all this abundance, it was not enough for Gregarion's children. Behind closed doors they began to plot against each other. The first who would fall were his half demon spawns. They were weak and easy to manipulate. They would barter for their lives but in the end, they would become a free meal for his greater children. The stronger of them began segregating themselves based on their bloodlines and revitalized the old ways of the republic. In the perspective of having only one throne for each of the nine segments, the fought among themselves until only nine remained. Honour among remaining brothers was maintained and they reclaimed the throne room.

Nearing the end of their age, a special delivery found its way to the keep.

There had been rioting in the streets as a special envoy of caged caravans pulled by slaved Dornarians made its way through the town. It would stop before the temple where a dramatic display had been held.

The leaders had been called off their throne to receive their gift. They had captured a half angel. This moment had been the first in over one hundred years that a demon laid eyes on an angel. Not a single demon could recall or were even aware of the angels' existence. The angel had been offered up as a tribute to their leaders.

The leaders debated this gift and realized she may be the best bargaining chip for finding a new king. They had the caravan moved indoors and began building a small crane over the pit. When the crane had been readied, they removed the boulders and timber from the gate to hell. They built a simple cantilevered arm with a lowering chain, attached a wooden cross to the chain upside down, and strapped her to it.

"Any last words, my dear?" said one of the children.

"You will all fall. You will not survive unless you release me now. I am Adira, Queen of the Angelic Kingdom of Elysica. The heavens will not allow this event to go unpunished. My husband will…"

"Will what. Save you from this?"

The demon lashed her armour from her flesh and flayed her side. Adira let out a blood curdling scream. The demon then looked around the room.

"That's right. He'll do nothing. Lower her in!"

Adira screamed as she was lowered into hell. Within minutes, her scream became a cry for help. Then, the only sound she made was a gurgle of blood before growing silent.

The chain began to shake. The crane began to twist and fell into the pit. A hand reached out and grabbed the rim. Rammathan rose from the pit. He was the strongest demon to ever emerge from the abyss, much greater than the malevolent lords of old, and far greater than the tainted blood of Gregarion's offspring. After taking in his first breath of mortal air, he sat on the throne.

The other demons approached Rammathan to admire their new King. Rammathan rose from his chair and tore six of them limb from limb without a shred of reaction from being attacked by the rest. He looked to the remaining three.

"Treachery, Anger, Deceit, you only live because I have use for you. You will serve me as my tribunal. Indulge me. Where am I and how vast does my kingdom grow?"

They spent their first year under his rule occupied by feeding him information. He would walk through the streets unchallenged and witnessed the city he has come to rule. In that time, he would learn of their history, the mechanics of life within a mortal plane and the function of their city as it existed in their day.

His entire stay had been plagued by one thought alone. He had a taste for angel flesh. Ever since he feasted on Adira, he thought of all the ways he could enjoy sadistically treating his old enemies on a mortal plane. As his stay continued, he devised manners and strategies that could lead to an inevitable victory.

In the last twenty years of his rule, he had been modifying Dornar's structure to become militant and rebuilt the armies of old. Eventually he would meet with King Nobelan, King of Elysica, who just happened to be the son of his first meal. It was that day the Blood Plains War truly began.

*****

Journal Entry,

Moranda was quite the storyteller. It was amazing the kind of details she was capable of divulging. With this knowledge I would be able to understand the Dornarian population further. My travels to their towns continued, and I developed a heartened defense for their weaker, more vulnerable half. Syrenne and I decided to bring justice to the land. It was at this point we decided to call ourselves "The Minstrels of Murder".

Our travels continued. We continued to sing songs of the lost and wronged, spreading empathy and love to the darkest of corners of Dornar. In those instances where we felt there may be hope, we would continue into the bogs in search of the lost and attempt to rescue them. In the cases where they remained lost, we sought justice. We learned how to fight demons from the demons themselves who had been protecting their kin from Dornar. We were then given costumes so all would recognize us. The costumes were reinforced with strong leathers and woven with rare metals, and the blades were sharper than any other.

For a time we became lost in the darkness, too. Our moral compass had fallen south and we became enthralled with punishment over justice. The swamp itself began turning us. Even my language became more poetic, a personality shift brought on by the costume that had developed into a new persona. I would become the hands of poetic justice in the swamp, and I became feared by those who indulged in malice.

It was as if months rolled by within the swamps. We had almost forgotten our native land, where we would roam free in the plains among the beasts natural to this world. We had become obsessed with our conviction to the point of complete selflessness.

During our travels, we heard rumours of a boat made of flesh and bone, unlike any had ever seen. The possessor of the boat had abandoned it. It was rumoured that he belonged to the island of ash. We had been amused by this rumour and went to investigate.

The rumours were true and there it sat on the coast. A boat completely made of the ribs, bones and flesh of some mighty predator, its joints and seals were made of caked blood. Unfortunately there were no signs of its possessor.

We continued to search for this fabled resident of the ashen island, but we never found him. The odd thing was Syrenne and I agreed that we almost felt his presence as if he were stalking us and covering his trail to avoid being found. It was obvious that he had been covering his trails, as he made foolish attempts to brush away his tracks. Even with the brushing, it was obvious that he was only human.

Weeks more rolled by without an appearance of our guest. We paid no mind and continued on our business. If anything, Syrenne and I stepped up our performance in hopes that he would be watching and be impressed by our gifts. Every night we sat silent, hoping he would present himself.

Eventually we crossed paths with the stranger. Clothed in steel and black velvet, he appeared war torn and helpless yet I could hear it his pant. His heavy, lion-like breaths muttering a destined royalty among beasts proved that he would long outlive any armour that would sustain him in battle. His eyes were red as rubies, peering through the slit of his steel mask. His ghostly white hair was banging forward over the mask and covered by his black velvet hood. Even his skin was crusted and flaked as drought covered ash plains, and gray as thunder clouds.

At first, we could see him examine us through the mask. We did not know how he managed to sneak up on us, but he directly crossed our paths and stopped us in our tracks. He stepped forward slowly, bladed hands down and his posture relaxed as if to lessen the distress. As he approached, he... smelled us.

"You are human. Why would you want to traverse these swamps? Do you have any idea what means to feed on you in this forsaken swamp?"

"And you are... very dark and obviously ill-fitted for these swamps. Should you not at least be wearing boots?"

"That is my concern."

"And our fate is ours."

"Correction: Your fate is also my concern. It is not safe for your kind here. I will help you find your way back to the plains."

"No."

"What do you mean no?"

"We have chosen this, and in turn the land has chosen us. They need us."

"Need us? Do you know what kind of vile creatures live here?"

"No! It's a lie! They are not all vile! Some of them live in fear. Some of them even live in rebellion of their forefathers. We have learned that they have the capacity for love and peace. Please, don't force us to go. We can help them here."

"You are an interesting folk. I'll tell you what. I will let you stay but you have to promise me that you will not let them taint your heart. If it comes down to violence, let me wield the hands of fate. A fist of judgement is not your call to make. Leave it to me."

"Who are you?"

"I am Benneth Aldercaine, and I am a chaosblood."

*****

Paradigm
Island of Ash

Paradigm, Island of Ash

As a chaosblood, I can tell you this. Nobody ventures to Paradigm. Not now, not ever. Not even the parents of those forsaken.

Long ago, when angels and demons first began inhabiting the land, they learned they had the ability to procreate with the humans. Why this would ever happen is a marvel of nature, but from what I take from it is that we were all created with the same cast, just created in different ways and in different places.

Despite the obvious, it started as a blessing and evolved into a plague. Half demons and half angels were having children, either from a half angel falling in love with a half demon, or a half demon having their way with a half angel. The circumstance of the event was inconsequential, but the result was this: Chaosbloods were being birthed into the world.

One of the leaders long ago decreed that chaosbloods could not be trusted. Either they would be too "good natured" to live among demons or too "parasitic and unknowable" to live among angels. So rather than exiling them elsewhere so they may fend for themselves, they took it as a potential conflict for those they would reside with. They simply spat them out into desolation.

Along the shores of Draemoria, their parents were forced to sail off the isle of Paradigm and launch their children on rafts toward the coast. If the child was given supplies, they were lucky. Many of these children never even survived the trip to shore. Fortunately for some, they would not be discovered until their youth where their more dominant features would then make them noticeable. At least as a youth they benefitted from life skills. Every chaosblood would be endowed gifts of a peculiar nature caused by the blending of the two bloods coalescing into a specific trait that would make them stand out among their kin. These gifts and prior knowledge would aid in their survival.

Paradigm was an island brewed from a fault line. Over time, the ash, cinder and magma bubbled out, making solid ground. The land was rich in nutrients, but little to no foliage could survive its wicked terrain. The only beasts that lived there were carnivores. How they arrived there no one knows, but most of them could not be seen anywhere else.

Survival on Paradigm without wisdom was bleak at best. With such an open terrain, beasts and children alike could be seen for miles with very few terrain aids. The only chaosbloods to survive this experience were properly gifted with either equipment or beneficial gifts given by blood.

I myself am an interesting story. I am Half Angel, Half Demon. My existence is purely coincidence. In a world where angels and demons have found their way to coexist among humans, over centuries their blood has crossed through children born of human blood. I was an extremely rare case where my parents, half angel and half demon, managed to pass on their angel and demon blood without a trace of human blood.

My mother was a simple farmhand in the Elysican flood plains, surrounded by lush fields of wheat and barley. A child with my abnormalities, having skin as ashen flakes, was found out very early in childhood. My mother attempted to hide me by raising me in the house as a scribe but it was no use. Eventually I would need sunlight and eventually someone would see me running in it. My mother was forced to sail to Paradigm alone and cast me into the oceans on a small raft. The violent creatures of the deep circled my raft but did not partake. I was lucky.

When I landed on Paradigm, I had barely any goods with me. I had enough bread and fish for the trip, and no skills to aid in gathering or hunting. Fortunately, I was found and raised by one of the oldest of chaosbloods. He managed to survive into his adolescence with great guidance. He never told me his name, though. I don't think he even had one.

He bore a great suit of armor, and grafted hand blades to his wrists that would allow him to fight to the death. His blades were unique. It appeared as though he welded two blades to each of his gauntlets. The blades were mounted on either side of the wrists, and the blades themselves were hooked near the hands. I can see why he designed them this way. He would use them to grapple with his enemy, catching their claws between the blades and twisting in such a way the blades would cleave their appendages. The hooks on the blades would aid him in catching wild swings or catching at different angles. His entire martial art was focused on the blades themselves. He eventually taught me how to fight this way by making my own fist weapons using leather and bone from his fallen victims.

Unfortunately, poor circumstance led to my learning of a gift to step into an alternate plane. We were hunting for food one day rather than fishing. My master felt it best that we would slay predators together so he can guide me through combat. Our predator had the advantage. There were more of them.

We were weaving through the ash made smoke stacks that spewed soot into the air. Most of them were no more than ten feet tall, but several of them could be much larger. The predators favoured this area since it provided camouflage and cover. We thought we were striking a weak one down. It had been mauled by a much larger beast and was whimpering for an end. We approached it in pity and that's when they struck as if they were planning on our arrival.

Seven of these beasts rushed my master and began to tear him limb from limb. They chased me down, but luckily I tried to jump into a swell but ran into the side of it instead. Rather than running into it and falling to the ground, I had crossed through. I was in a parallel world. It looked exactly like our world, but the sky was filled with stars. There was no moon and no sun. The land was flooded with an eerie, unnatural light, just enough to see but too little to provide any real definition or depth. Where shadows should be, I saw the living world, the world where I belonged. I was looking into a mirror.

I could see the beasts feeding on my master's corpse down to the bone. They left nothing but metal plates. They even pulled the flesh of his hands from his weapons. Eventually they moved on. I could see them travelling into the distance from numerous shadows away. I could see for miles there. After they had left, I tried to step through into the living world again. It was like walking through a door. The two worlds were seamless. I reclaimed my master's gear and brought them into this parallel plane with me.

Rather than living in Paradigm, I utilized this gift and remained in this alternate plane where there was no life. The world was absolutely barren except for the bones of beasts that had stuck out of the ground and were as stiff as stone. They had been there for ages and there was no sign of immediate life. At first I used this gift to hunt, simply ambushing the beasts as they slept. I didn't even need to leave the shadow. I learned that I could make fires in the shadows, and it never altered the gateways. Fires in the living world sealed them up. My gift was tied to the living world.

I began to tan the hides of my prey and use them to piece together my master's armour. I also began building practice dummies to reinforce the martial art my master had been teaching me. I never became fully confident in my combat prowess, since his training was never completed, but it was more than enough when companied with my gift.

I realized I had become the alpha of this land and became bored of the monotony of survival. I figured there must be more to life than a never ending loop of hunting. I began to build a stockpile of bones and leather. I also learned that mixing animal blood with ash made a sort of black pitch. Using the dried out, buoyant animal bones, I built the framework for a raft, lined it with hides and sealed it in blood pitch within the shadows.

Then I would face the real test. I would have to kill a ferocious beast, one with skins large enough to make a gate. I began scouring the shadows in search of such a beast. Then I found it. It was a hideous reptile, well over twenty feet tall and with eight legs. It was monstrously muscular and its scales appeared to be sharp as daggers. I figured I would bait it.

I began moving from the smoke stacks and toward the beast, remaining in the shadows, and dropping meat in the living world. I formed a trail that eventually led to the home of the beast. The beast began to sniff. It turned and saw me. It ran for me, looking at me like the meal of a lifetime. I jumped into the shadows and it began flailing around, thinking that I had jumped at it. After it came to rest, it began eating the meat. It then began following the meat trail. Once it was in the smoke stacks, there was no escape.

I waited for it to relax and lay for a nap. At that moment, I jumped out of the shadow and hamstringed its rear legs. It coiled back and let out a shriek then stammered to its feet. It began to circle and defend itself again. It was hopeless. I would leap out and strike at its legs then return to the shadows before it could even make a movement. As I fought, I noticed its own shadow had been deceiving it. I began clawing and sawing at its feet every opportunity it would afford me until it was in too much pain to stand. When it began to lay down is when I began to strike its vitals. Eventually it would submit and it passed away.

It would take some time, but I managed to flay the flesh from the corpse. I dragged it into the shadows using its own shadows. I dragged it to shore where my boat rested. I had to fight with a smaller shadow to get it back to the living world. That took me a while, but it happened. I used it as a tarp and made a lean-to with bones for support, and then dragged the boat into the living world. From there, I sailed back to the main land.

From what I have said, that is all anyone would probably ever learn of Paradigm. There was no culture, no community, not even a population. My master had been the only one to survive long enough to meet me, and during my stay I rarely, if ever, saw a boat from a mainland. Most of the chaosbloods cast here would die in the ocean.

That was probably the most disturbing part of my stay. The waters never tested my boat. Not even the creatures below me. Then I recalled my journey here. Even then the creatures would swim along my raft. It was like they had accepted me as the alpha of their world.

At first I didn't even care about my destination. I just figured I would plot a generally east course that would save the boat from damaging tides and weather. My concern was more of surviving the trip. When my trip had ended, my boat found rest on the shores of Dornar.

My first reaction was to run for cover and enter the shadows. Dornar was perfect for its canopy enveloped the land. I could move in and out of the shadows at will and any time. I began spying on Dornar to see the truth behind their culture. There was no culture, just an endless, parasitic and chaotic chain of feeding on vice and vanity. It was disgusting. They were even rounding up humans as livestock and play toys.

I still considered my boat as base camp so that I could keep my bearings on the land. Every so often I would return. Obviously my visits were too often because Dornarians had picked up my scent. They began spreading rumours of my existence, and that's when I would encounter the most intriguing of people yet.

Sorrownote and Syrenne had found their way to my boat and had examined its build. It appeared to make Syrenne nauseous, but Sorrownote was intrigued by the craftsmanship. They had found my trails. A solid month it had been since I set foot on the surf and still. They had found my trail.

I began to follow them. Even in the living world. Hiding among the shadows lacked grace. I wanted to clue them into my presence. After a while of fun and games, and witnessing their overall good nature, I decided to approach them and make my presence known. From there, we became friends.

Over time and through several encounters with my newly discovered, good willed friends, I had figured out that my gift of moving into the shadows wasn't a gift of living in the shadows at all. On an island filled with beasts, the terrain of the shadow plane seemed desolate. Now that I resided on the mainland, I realized its true nature. I had been Purgatory, where he walks among the dead at the moment the world had ceased to live.

I began piecing the concept together when I first arrived. Back on Paradigm, all was petrified as if it had been there ages. When I entered the shadows in the mainland, all life was rotting. Not even molds were alive. It was just a chain of decay that went on forever. Life had simply ceased. I eventually told Moranda of my story, and she used herbs to run some tests on me. That is when I had found out that I had no human blood. My soul had become so conflicted that I was torn between the two worlds, and shot into infinity where I managed to reach the end of time.

There came a time when our journeys in the swamp, while vanquishing a Dornarian that had slain an innocent victim, we were approached by three angels and a demon. It was a very odd company, and I embellished the tone of my introduction to see how they would react to my existence as a chaosblood. It seemed to weird them a bit, but the demon looked excited.

As Sorrownote mentioned, my demonic blood had provided me with a subtle sense of smell that could tell me the very makeup of a person's blood.

One of the angels and the demon were not angel and demon. They were human, but contaminated with a strong dose of light and darkness, as if they had been imbued with pure essence. I didn't want to say anything at first, but Moranda confirmed it.

They seem excited to see Moranda again. All I have to say is pure angels are amusingly delightful. I enjoyed travelling around them. Their very presence was uplifting, like they could heal the swamps just by setting foot in it. It was an experience like no other. I would continue to follow this band to the ends of the earth. I would protect them with my life. My life had now been given purpose. After her tests and incantations, Moranda divulged a plot from Dornar. It was planning a massive scale attack on Elysica. She didn't know when or where, but it either had to be prepared for or stopped. This is when we decided to take our corners to warn our people, and the demon Joseph and I were best suited to deal with Dornar. I requested that Joseph would travel with me. My previous experiences in Dornar would aid me.

In the shadows, Dornar was unique. It is then that I learned that souls could drift off into eternity, not finding a fate in the heavens or in the abyss, simply anchored to the world with no future. Time became timeless and they would continue to walk along the rotting terrain. Their faces were gone and they had no distinguishable features. I attempted to communicate with them but none of them would even respond to my gestures. I could not even move them. They were frozen in time and yet could wander by themselves. I was then confronted by a group of these denizens and they were capable to speak.

They warned me of the coming war by giving me a piece of paper. The piece of paper read the fate of the world, and I was told that it was the last page in the book of its life. The page read;

> *Today is the day I feel the world will end. King Rammathan had managed to storm Elysica Keep and vanquish Nobelan in pure hatred. There was no cause, no disruption, just a bloodthirsty ambition to slay everything good in this world. His demons were forever slaying the angels, even to the best of their ability, the angels had fallen. The gates to heaven have closed themselves in the anguish of a lost plane, and preventing Rammathan and his minions from stepping through. It has been a week since the trumpets*

had sounded, and there were no sided kings left to answer the call. Rammathan and his minions kept feeding on the people. There are no humans left save for us. Nobelan managed to hide us in a passage that had an escape vessel waiting for us. We had sailed for the Hall of Great Kings in an attempt to save this land. I am afraid it's too late. The War Lock will make this world fall. He will clean up the mess that should have never been. The world is over. I just wish I could live long enough to hand this to....

And the last page ended abruptly. The War Lock, sitting at the end of time, had found this journal. He was reading it when he began reading of me. That is when he handed this page to these denizens to deliver to me, right here in this very spot. They claim that even this quote I am writing now was contained in this journal. It had amused him because the words had looped itself, once in my writing as I am writing now, and once at the end of time.

What amuses me is Sorrownote never reads these stories. He is so preoccupied with gathering our stories and writing stories of his own that he never actually reads anything. I wonder if he will write of this one day, or if he will ever know that his book lived to the end of time. What interests me now is how this book will end. If we change the fate of this world, this part of time just happened. These writings are still here. Will the War Lock still get a hold of this book? I wonder.

At the time we entered Dornar, I was not aware of its condition and we happened to be on the east end, which pit us against Anger. Fortunately for Joseph, it wasn't violence. Anger is a much different trait, one more self-involved, and the demons were more concerned about themselves and others than at some random wanderers. I would tell him to run through the land, and I began to use my gift to slay whatever stood in his path. It was a pleasurable feat, jumping from shadow to shadow, delivering killing blows to demon after demon. I did not enjoy killing, but the feat itself was challenging and amusing. What interested me, the fallen demons within Purgatory would disappear. As I slayed them, they no longer existed within Purgatory. Mind you, not all of them existed there in the first place. My guess is that they had moved on before the end of time came. But the ones that did. Their bodies would simply vanish as if they were erased from time. It could not be Purgatory, for their soul was not trapped. They simply did not live long enough to become trapped. It was just the end of time, and time had halted.

I would love to continue on this story for you, but apparently Sorrownote has plans for the current matters. He asked me to go as far as necessary to explain where I come from and this last dose of knowledge is my end. I will leave you on this note, and hope you have pleasure in reading Sorrownote's interpretation of what happens next.

*****

Journal Entry,

On our travels with Benneth, we came across the most unlikely band of travelers. We saw three angels paired with a demon. After introductions, we have found two of the angels to be the future rulers of Elysica. They were named Lord Adrian Arias and Lady Lorelei Arias. The other two claimed to be humans from Belliscia that had been changed into angels and demons. Their names were Joseph and Jennifer.

We eventually found the opportunity to ask Joseph and Jennifer while visiting Moranda for her tests. I had asked Joseph and Jennifer to indulge me in the history of Belliscia. Joseph was a mayor's assistant. He lived to be his errand boy and was privy to some knowledge. His penmanship was refined, so I managed to get him to begin writing his story. His conversational skills were still very juvenile but he managed to get the just of his story on paper.

Jennifer had lived in a mausoleum her entire life and been learning from knowledge constructs. Apparently these constructs had been teaching her, but they could not shed much light on their land or even anything negative about it. It was as if the constructs were preserving her purity even in context. She was carrying crystals that she had taken from their remains after Joseph cleaved them apart. They must have been from Mechanus.

There was something odd about this couple. Well, they weren't couples at first, but they were bound to become one. They didn't have the same presence about them as an angel or demon. Even Benneth noted that they didn't "smell" like angels or demons. In its strange truth, I could see what he was saying. They were just people. If anything, they appeared lost and hopeless. Over time their position had grown on them, but you can still see the frail human spirit that lay beneath their skin.

Beyond the physical, both of them were relatively simple. I could see if Joseph hadn't become a mayor's assistant, he would have probably become farm hands. Every gesture and every mannerism about him was simple. Belliscians were known for living in bliss and ignorance. Not that ignorance would be a bad word in their case. Ignorance simply meant they would enjoy living without the need for knowledge of the rest of the world. Joseph was different, though, he seemed to take in everything he witnessed and even jumped into conversation. He aspired to adventure and loved obtaining stories of the world beyond Belliscia.

Unfortunately for Jennifer, she lived in a mausoleum her entire life. She didn't even remember how she got there. It was a pity, for her only recollection would be of the teachings of soulless robots. Even then the robots would only divulge very specific knowledge. Everything about Jennifer was pure and simple, as if she had been preserved in an absolutely pure state. Her travels had opened her eyes to the real world, and at first it appeared distressing to her. I think she has realized the impact she could make upon it, and she is beginning to embrace mortality. She had also been given gifts which not even the angels can comprehend. We still don't know where they came from, neither Joseph's gifts for that matter.

*****

Belliscia, Island of Serenity

Hello, I am Joseph from Belliscia and I have been asked to tell you a story. Sorrownote believes my influence in Belliscia and the wisdom I have gained from being in its government fabric would be a benefit, so who am I to refuse. My demonic form must have deceived him in first impressions. I was not always a demon. I am actually a child in my hometown. I have only begun working in office a few years back. I was found to have the aptitude for the position beyond my years. I just think I studied more than the rest. I found knowledge inspiring and intriguing. Most of the other children just wanted to work or play.

A dramatic event turned me into this demon and that's why we are now here. Hopefully Moranda can cure me. If not, well, we have a long road ahead of us because I am not stopping until I am human again. Being a demon is upsetting. Not to mention I have a thing for Jennifer. Being a demon doesn't help when you feel romantic about an angel.

Belliscia was founded 50 years into the reign of angels and demons. A meeting was called with the representative at his tower, and he presented an option to our tribe. He told us that we could move to this island which he called Belliscia. The angels had already started building docks, and the representative himself had influence within Mechanus and managed to have a dock built on the island. It still stands to this day, except we barely use it for anything other than fishing. We don't even trade with the mainland very often. They do, however, make stops once every so often just to check up on us and make casual trade to keep the lines open.

In the beginning, we were still a tribe. We had a feeling that this world would become a mess and even our home would eventually be stripped from us. It hurt to leave our kin, but it was necessary. We wanted to preserve our way of life and live in peace. There were many boats made available, but they could not carry more than a few dozen people. There were about 300 of us in all in the beginning, and it took a few days to move us and all of our supplies.

The Stalker's Fangs and Bear's Paws were the first to scuttle across the ocean and disembark the boats. When their boats had docked and they set foot on the mainland, they paid homage to their new land by burning fine herbs provided by the Rabbit's Foot. They would smear their ashes on their faces and arms for protection and to radiate a peaceful disposition that would calm the beasts. The Bear's Paw would set up camp on the shore to protect the docks as the Stalker's Fang would investigate the remainder of the island.

It was true. Belliscia was perfect in harmony. It had a peaceful forest, animal life, and a vast plain. The land was rich and the air was crisp. There were no predators on the island, and the beasts were many. We realized then we would no longer need to be nomads.

Belliscide had not yet become what it is today, but the first settlement that would become Belliscide was then founded. After all the remaining people had arrived, they assembled their provisions and beasts of labour along the coast where they would be safe. The people were then guided around the island by the Stalker's Fang. They would take in all that the land had offered and found a peace beyond any they had ever witnessed. The people were delighted and began to decide where they would make their home.

They had found the perfect spot. Near center yet off to the west, there was a nook in the west and north tree lines. This nook bordered the vast plains that filled most of the central island, and was substantially higher than the coast line. From there, Belliscia would have vantage of all the sorts of terrain that made their island so beautiful. The people began digging sticks in the ground and marking them with their tribe. They began making claim to where they would build their homes. Each tribe had a different impression of what was true natural beauty and wished to have the view and access to their preferred features.

The tribes then returned to the coast where their supplies remained untouched. The island was truly secluded. They would lead their beasts to their home and began setting up camp. As they unpacked, they noticed the angels had planted tools among their supplies with pictograms showing them how to use them. There had been plows, rakes, hammers, chisels, and more. Rather than setting them aside as our old kin would, we figured living in a new land may provide a new opportunity and we decided to keep them for future use.

By nightfall, the local animal life began watching them from the forest. The Rabbit's Foot, preferring the tree line, took note and slowly approached the animals bearing gifts of herbs and berries. The animals would slowly step into the clearing, and ate from the hands of the Rabbit's Foot. It was taken that the land would reciprocate their delight in presence.

That night, the tribes all sat around the same campfire and began deciding who would form their council. The council would then live among the people since it was pointless to create a separate tribe for them. After long deliberation, the first order of the council was to decree "The natural residents of this land are off limits for hunting. They had embraced us and we embrace them in return. We will return to Elysica and request provision of feeding livestock."

Several of our people went back to the docks and requested passage to Elysica. When they arrived, the angels gave them more provision with joy in their hearts. They handed us plenty of livestock and grain to get started. They knew the land was meant for preservation, but our hearts grew and matured in the new land. Eventually our people would be relaxed like the Elysicans.

In time our governing system fell away. We felt no use for a council. Yet again, we went to the Elysicans and asked for more suited guidance. Over a short period of time, the angels told us of several civilizations that had blossomed across the universe and how they had structured their government. We enjoyed and embraced the concept of democracy, and this led to having a mayor's office and local senate.

We also began to advance our skills in all aspects and our civilization prospered. We began to build fully functioning structures, houses, offices and even market places. We took great investment in preserving what we built. Even to this day you will find people oiling the cedars of their walls.

With the advent of Elysican influence on our people, there was bound to be demonic presence. Human nature is always conflicted by its choices, whether richer or poorer, and it would be inevitable for those to seek temptations and desires.

A few of our own began building fishing vessels that had been secretly smuggling supplies into Belliscide. A few of them would be persecuted for their items, but some less harmful substances such as distilled spirits and ales were allowed. Anything contradictory to the preservation of life would be sent back to Dornar, and even some would be banished from the island.

From there, Belliscide became pretty much what it is today. We tend to gloat of the bliss that we live in, without connection to the "silly world" beyond our shores, but they play a much larger role in our lives than we like to confess.

Our current Mayor, Mayor Winston, is actually from Mechanus. He was one of the few humans to have no alterations whatsoever and was from the world of Mechanus. He figured he'd give a shot at office and our people were entertained by the notion of having such a person leading them. A person with all that advanced knowledge and wisdom may have some benefit for them.

I served him for about five years, ever since I left finishing school. He handpicked me. I don't know why to this day. I know I had a gift as a scribe but I was much more rebellious and free willed than the rest of my class mates. In the old times I would've probably ended up a Horse's Mane.

I wish I could carry on for you, but Belliscia is just this simple. I hope you enjoyed what I had to say.

*****

Journal Entry,

Lorelei and Adrian was a couple made in heaven. As we sat inside with Moranda, they just sat in the tree picking herbs together. I did not want to disturb, and we ended up getting into the thick of business. I managed to talk to them at the end of the war as we arrived in Elysica for our celebration party.

Elysica was unlike any land I had ever witnessed. Its tall, ivory tower surrounded by miles of pristine built homesteads, a port with great merchant ships and an order and refinement to every facet of their land. Their people lived in complete peace and humility. Their children would play in the streets without a care or fear. They were completely enthralled by love. Lorelei and Adrian reflected this radiance, and it seemed to give them life as we walked through it. Don't let my words deceive you. They did not preserve a docile culture. They had knights that could not be compared to.

The Elysican Knights had donned great plates of white jade and ivory, trimmed with silver and ivory. They even claimed their armour was harder than steel. Apparently they found a way to coat them by using gigantic oysters. They even inlaid pearls and trimmed the armour in gold. Their weapons were of the greatest refine, their blades represented a quick painless resolve. They believed that if justice must be absolute, it should not bear any sign of wrath, for delivering pain out of spite was wickedness. Their shields would be more valuable to them than their swords. The shields would allow them to bide time to weaken and wind their foes, for most attacks were attacks blind with anger and an exhausted foe was more likely to realize their faults. They only struck when absolutely necessary. Several of them also donned bows and arrows that would be used in the most heated of battles. When lives were at stake, angels would not sacrifice a single mortal life. They would execute their foes with precision.

*****

The Angelic Kingdom of Elysica

The Angelic Kingdom of Elysica

Well, Lorelei and I, Adrian, are easily agreeable, so we decided that I would speak of heaven, since my role in heaven functioned within heaven, and Lorelei would speak of Elysica, since her role was inspiration among the people. Since we are from heaven, she had given me the right to start the introductions. I believe she still plans on introducing herself. Perhaps she will explain a few things in her writing. I will be reading this after. I hope she doesn't read this before. "Honey, if you are reading this, please, continue to write it. I wouldn't mind reading the explanation. Thanks." You will get that later on, and so will I, hopefully.

Anyway, where was I. Oh, yes. Heaven. You will love that place, well, I hope you do one day. The other place is just revolting. Anyway, heaven was so enjoyable because of me. Well, because of our Creator, but I had a good hand in it for mortals among angels. I was an angel of ecumenical politics. For those uneducated in such a term, that means my job was to audit and sort heaven.

Long ago, our creator decreed for those who would end up in heaven, heaven would be as they wished it on the earth. In other words, my job was to make your heaven just like you wanted it. To you, that may sound like a very tenuous job. To me, it was my daily bread.

I would spend my days sorting the souls of all mankind across several dimensions of any given moment. If you died and your soul was ready to be received, I had to have a comfortable nook waiting for you. Oh, but wait. What if your idea of heaven wasn't like another's? Or even, what if your idea of heaven didn't include another? We all embrace forgiveness and live like one big happy family up here, but unfortunately since the decree, people had the right to divide each other. Even if they had the right to salvation and a "get in heaven free" card, they still had the right to maintain their bitterness between each other, or maintain differences in opinion. So that's when the "shake hands or part" clause came into effect.

We all know that everyone gets a free ticket to heaven. All they have to do is take it. Some don't believe as such. Some believe that you had to live an entire life of good and servitude just to get here. They tended to segregate themselves and it ended up not being a happy place to be and heaven is all about happy. So we made some rules. Let's just let them sort themselves.

So my office was instated. My job was to make it so certain people could see certain people, the things that they experienced would be the things they wanted to experience and the things they didn't simply didn't exist for them. For instance, you know the whole 'wine' thing in heaven? Yeah, there are entire cultures that don't indulge in that treat. Gone!

I spent an eternity sorting souls to make heaven perfect, and it was perfect. I loved my job. I would get up every morning, walk to work, arrive at my massive tower of an office, sit at my beautiful desk for as long as needed until I was allowed to leave, then party with the mortal souls. There were so many cultures across the planes and so many of them got along. Even the ones that didn't were still enjoyable because their heaven remained intact. If only they knew what I did. Well, let's just hope that never happens.

So, you can imagine, heaven itself is extremely complex. It has all the greatest and beautiful of all kingdoms of all the dimensions all bound into one immaculate landscape. Those with the open eye can take in its complete grandeur. I have to say, sitting in an office is a luxury because if I continually had my breath taken away I would feint. My days off are the best. I use them just to venture among all the different cultures. There is only one word to describe the experience, and it is love. Pure love.

I also had the most beautiful and imaginative wife in the universe. Her name was Lorelei. Our creator created us at the beginning of time, from the light, and made several of us in twos. Our creator flew solo. I couldn't grip that and so couldn't He. He found it in his best interest to create us in twos so we could live with each other for an entire eternity. He even made our personalities in complement so it would never get dry. It never has! I still love her to this day and I will continue to the end of eternity.

She was a gift of inspiration. She would go from home to home, timeless, and in an instant inspire billions of minds across galaxies and dimensions. It was amazing to see. She would never share what she had woven, though. She enjoyed leaving it for a surprise, picking out highlights for me to witness. I had the pleasure of seeing poets, artists and musicians, engineers, diplomats and speakers blossom from the most unforeseeable corners of their worlds. They would be given such a passion that they would shape their world for generations to come. Lorelei took pride in making one simple act ripple through civilizations, and those ripples would perpetuate through time itself.

Are there other angels? Well, there are entire choirs of angels! We were all one, big, happy family. Our purposes, though, weighted us into position. It just seemed logical that certain circles would be given precedence in heaven, so we agreed to it. We had three primary choirs.

One choir would represent our creator and his voice, maintaining and protecting the throne, and stood for justice and resolution. Very few of them ever mixed with the masses, but their voice could carry through the entire kingdom. Being the first of us, our creator also blessed them with heavenly voices, and they could sing for the span of eternity. Lots of the songs were written to glorify the throne. Hey, if you invented music, I mean, the person who thought of an idea called music, I bet the first song you would write is "I made music! I'm so awesome!" He SPOKE light into existence. He gave us life. I think that's pretty awesome.

They were so strong in their position they would never budge. Can you imagine being at the ready for all of eternity? These guys were intense. They were also the ones on the front line when the deceiver built the revolt. It is said he was one of them and decided to relinquish his position. Even to this day he loves using his voice to deceive and warp humanity. That topic is a little upsetting for this moment. We'll talk about that later.

The second choir would lead in government and regulation, and our job was to lead, collaborate and claim authority over the other angels in order to preserve the heavens and its integrity. Our first leader among mortals, Theocrites, was one of us. It was his duty to maintain a governing position among humanity when time served right.

It was in this effect, my charge to sort the heavens to protect its integrity for all who abode within it. We all had many parts to fulfill though, even as peacekeepers and warriors. No, the protectors were not the only ones to be trained in combat. Sure, the first of us to form the Elysican travelers would be chosen from the highest choir as high guards, but we were offensive. It was our job to keep it going, to govern and defend against the wickedness that may unfold.

The third choir would serve among the mortals, being our soldiers, messengers, and embracers, such as Lorelei who would serve as inspiration. They took on many forms, but it's these angels that would be the ones mortals would most often perceive. Many of the other choirs were dedicated to function within heaven itself, and every few ever engaged in contact with the human world. It just wasn't their place. If the other choirs were asked to do something in the mortal worlds, they would just send these angels on their behalf. I know it sounds like a 'pass the buck' deal, but it was all in purpose.

Mortals were different in creation, though. Being his second series of creations, he had more time invested and they were his favourite. It didn't really bother us. He tasked us in watching out for them, for they were frail and mortal, and once their time had ended in their plane they would join us in eternity, but that was it. So, we took the charge with glee and enjoyed every moment of it.

Unfortunately, one of us decided to divide the heavens. He felt that the mortals were getting more love and we deserved more, that we had great gifts and he challenged the greatest throne of all for the right to rule for himself. He began spreading rumours that started a riot, and he was casted into the abyss. It was the furthest place from the heavens imaginable, and lacked our source of life. The problem was, with his hatred he began using his gift in rebellion, pitting man against his creator and turning the mortal worlds sour. It began to make us sad. I think that was his intention.

We never gave up. It became part of our mandate to watch out for these souls during their mortal stay. And we did, until one day a portal opened.

It was odd. We were given the gift to speak into their lives and watch over them, every so often given the ability to take on presence within their worlds, but we could never actually live among them. Our creator must have felt this one particular world worth the gift, and so opened a gate where we could cross over.

We deliberated and decided who would go through. They were some of our wisest and strongest, those who could make the greatest impact in the shortest amount of time. The rest of us just watched as their culture began to flourish. It was like music, and we are all about music.

Our people continued to cross into their world for over a hundred years. Less and less became tempted to cross as they had learned that the angels had also become mortal, but they have also found love among the mortals. It was said that love as a mortal was incomparable in heaven. So, angels continued crossing, but only those with enough will to tempt fate. When it was learned that demons lived among them, the temptation became less because we had learned of our ability to die and be killed. We would eventually return to heaven, but as mortals we would return as souls. Our creator gave us an incomparable gift, but it is a gift to ponder over since we would never return as angels.

Then it happened. One day my beautiful wife had set a nice ring next to my breakfast. It was made of gold and had a ruby carved with a sigil. It was like what the humans would use as a signet ring to brand documents with wax. I loved it! She knew I would. Thanks honey!

Days passed and I started dreaming. I would dream of armies, one in white jade armour and one in obsidian armour, slamming into each other, then my vision was flooded with light. I would then see an angel, but an angel like no other, and she was singing. Then I would see my signet ring spinning in open space. I don't know about you, but to me, a recurring dream like that is just unnatural.

One day, on my way out of the house and on my way to work, Lorelei stopped me.

"Please don't go. I don't feel right about today. Let's just stay home and cuddle."

"Feel wrong? In heaven? Nonsense. I'll be home before you know it."

"Can I at least come along with you? Until you get to the office. I promise I will get back to the field, making dreams for mortals right after."

And that's when it happened. Oh, no. We didn't get to choose to walk through the gates. We got chosen. This next part is probably the only part in the history of parts that bothers me about being mortal, the fact that we didn't get to choose. Yeah, I got over it, but still. Come on.

So, the sky started to turn red. I rubbed my eyes. Yep. The sky started to turn red. It got really windy. Wind in heaven? Yep, real wind. Then my signet ring released a little ball of red... red. It was just a ball of red. It was kind of like a marble. Then it went flat. It became a floating red disk of red. The red disk of red then became a gigantic floating red disk of red that was taller than me. It then started to grow a hand, a hand of red protruding from a floating red disk of red. Is anyone else getting this? It then grew and arm. Ok I'll stop with the embellishment.

The hand then reached out and grabbed Lorelei and I in one fell swipe and sucked us into the red disk of red. Then I blacked out. You would think I would've redded out, but I am not mistaken, I definitely blacked out.

We woke up in a hay bail. Our heads were killing us. My God, we had pain. Angels don't get pain, but we were feeling pain. What was happening to us?

We found out that we were in the stables when we were met by a stableman. When we woke up, they began calling for aid. God, its shrill voice still echoes in my brain to this day, probably because the experience was traumatizing on top of my already existent headache. Feeling time in sequence was a very interesting experience.

We were then led to our new king, King Nobelan. We had found out he was the long descendant of Theocrites, and we resided almost two hundred years since the opening of the gates. This amazed me because I remember watching this land in its infancy, and I knew plenty about it and its people. I also knew about our new neighbours.

I was told that the signet ring I was bearing would make me the future king of this land. There's the kicker! I had a golden ticket to be a king among mortals, but I would be mortal myself. I eventually got over it, but it's been a fabulous run.

We had been tasked with becoming rangers, basically long distance runners who would come to aid for those we were tasked with. Most of our tasks entailed guidance, tracking, and gathering. We loved it, because it gave us the opportunity to invest in the lives we already were tasked in impacting from heaven. It was intended to give us a reputation for our future rule, but we didn't take it that way. We also spent plenty of time in the keep alongside King Nobelan, where we would learn of our new position and our duties to come. Now we have been here 10 years. His most current charge brought us here.

So, that pretty much sums up to current events, and now on to Lorelei with the history.

Well, I'm supposed to be inspiration, so I gifted him with a coy personality. Isn't he a doll? Well, he would like to know how he got his ring, and I know it has been bothering him. So here it is.

While we were in heaven, I really did just intend on giving him a gift. This signet ring was a sign of affection. The big gold ring with a nice ruby carved into a sigil looked distinguished among everything else the pawn broker was carrying. Wait, now. I remember the pawn broker. He was the stableman that called for assistance! We had been duped! We knew that it would be possible to re-enter heaven, but we decided to stay. Yes, we did not like the idea of not choosing, but our first notion was we were chosen for our position and we are perfect for it so it just worked out for us. We are the first angels on this planet in over a hundred years so yes they need new angel blood among them to instill some freshness into its system. We are a pair so we will sire descendants of pure blood for them, and they will in turn become part of these people in two generations which is good to us. Do we wish to go back to heaven? Honestly? We've talked about it and we are now happy as mortals. We know our fate will one day make us mortal souls in heaven, but it doesn't sound like such a bad idea. With that being said, let's continue on with our story, shall we?

So, from the beginning I had been watching Elysica. I remember the first of the tribes that had entered the flood plains. They already knew a good portion of their land as nomads, but they had a calling to more. My first inspirations to the people were to pursue the light in order to reach their creator on a more personal level, and to pursue goodness among each other.

Eventually, the beliefs I instilled became worship, and they built a temple in the name of the light. They even called it "The Temple of Lights". Eventually, that worship led to a gate opening between our worlds. Since our plane is immortal and timeless, our deliberation went on for an age but appeared to be mere seconds to the humans. First, the greatest of our travelers stepped through. His name was Theocrites. He brought with him 24 of his favourite warrior angels to serve as his high guard, and plenty of artisans, tradesmen, philosophers and artists to teach the people. Though they had plenty of wisdom to share, Theocrites had instructed to not divulge any information but love and peace for the first ten years. We were supposed to know our people, down to their very hearts.

So we lived among the people in peace and tranquility. We lived among them as they lived, nomads on the plains, feeding off the grains. As we began to age, we also began to get sick in the first of the years. It was then we realized that we were also mortal, and began partaking in the flesh of beast to maintain our stamina. The thought of ending life did not agree with us at first, but then we recalled the purpose of simple life and how all creations were made in a circuit to allow life to thrive. We were now part of that circuit.

After our ten years, we began to teach the people. They already had a taste for culinary delight, but we had eons of knowledge from cultures across universe and the dimensions. We would show them dishes so succulent they would never allow their people to eat any less quality than we would teach them.

We also began to teach them domestication. At first, they had been hunting animals, following herds and taking what they needed to survive. We liked the idea of taking only what they needed. That was good. Needing to constantly travel and hunt was not good for the health of the community or for building a solid foundation. So, we taught them how to use many people and slight doses of fear to steer the herds, so they would go where they pleased rather than having to chase them down. Afterwards, we set up wooden fences high enough to trap beasts. We also built on fertile soil to perpetuate their need for food. After the animals were trapped, they would become docile. Larger beasts needed the ability to run and maintain their fitness, so we also taught the people of the proper sizes for these pens based on animal breed and number.

During domestication, something peculiar happened. The tribespeople showed the angels how they had befriended the wolves. The wolves of their world were unlike any other. They had humanlike personality traits and spoke to the tribespeople. Sure, their language wasn't overly formulated, but they would carry on conversation through their "Spirit Tongue" as it were. Rather than domesticating the wolves, the wolves would live among their population as equal and treated as kin. We delighted in this circumstance and welcomed them into our lives and homes. Wolves would become part of the community.

After a while, when the people got used to having their animals in one spot, we showed them how the animals were conscious beings. Their soothsayers already had an understanding for this, and had a rare gift to speak to the spirits within the animals. This claim is legitimate, and it is the first time we ever witnessed it among mortals. What we then did is teach them to communicate in a way that would ask them to help operate. The animals then willingly became beasts of burden, aiding with building and function within the community.

After domestication came agriculture. When it came to grains and plants, the people had a tendency to eat only what was available. During the winter season they became dependant on the meats. To that effect, we began teaching them about why the plants grew and how. We first traveled to all corners of their land, collecting a variety of fruits, vegetables, herbs and grains. We then taught them how to plant their seed in the soil. In a season, they began bearing fruit and they enjoyed the plentiful bounty they had reaped. It was at that moment we taught that their fruit would also contain seed so they could continue growing. They no longer needed to find their food. It was also important that those crops, like grains, would need to have a portion reserved for planting, since they would eat the seed, and the plants would also die in time and needed to be replaced.

In time, they would learn of crop rotation. The people had to learn that as plants provided different forms of nutrition, they would also withdraw that nutrition from the ground below them as they grew. Different plants would also return different forms of nutrition into the soil, and even more after decaying at the end of their life. Those new nutrients in the soil would now provide the nutrients necessary to grow other crops. We taught them of all these plants and how they would work together to sustain the earth below them, so that the plants could continue to grow as they did for future generations. We also taught them as their civilization would progress, they would eventually find more plants that would work within that system. The more plants they would grow, the more prosperous the soil would become in the right order.

Now that they had domestication and agriculture, and they were capable of thriving beyond their foreseen years, it was important to instill a trade system. The trade system that we had instilled placed a level of responsibility over their products rather than ownership or authority. The concept was to place the product in the care of the farmer. That farmer in turn would return to the community with its bounty in order to preserve life, in turn trade with the other farmers for their provision and the necessary amounts of seed for their next harvest rotation. This way, all people would get their fair share of a whole and there would be enough left over in the hands of those who cared for the seed to be able to perpetuate the cycle. The same process was instilled into the animal farmers, for they needed to continue trade between the communities so sickness from breeding within the same ilk would not develop.

Now, the people had domestication, agriculture and trade. After a good five years, the people felt ever grateful for what they have learned, and began investing in the Temple of Lights in order to say thank you to the heavens.

Theocrites then invested in the people and their trade skills. Great artisans among the angels began to inspire the people, and taught the people advanced secrets and methods of working with stone and steel, and how to form glass from the sands. They invested in all aspects of their trades, imbuing knowledge beyond their generations and sending them in a quantum leap forward in development. For some reason, the angels avoided technology, for they saw the potential hazards it would provide. Its use in the people could be beneficial, but humans had the tendency of not knowing when to stop, constantly trying to find the next step and destroying in its name. They would find ways around it, showing them satisfaction in the simpler pleasures of skill refinement rather than skill progression.

With the aid of the angels, they built a magnificent ivory tower, to represent a bridge between the heavens and the earth, that our people were now united. The main floor was divided into many large rooms with several seats and desks with different functions. We told them they were court rooms, and they did not understand what it meant. They were simple enough and beyond vice and did not need to know as of yet.

They also began to build the marketplace, where the primary trades would occur. The people would still trade among each other in the fields for provision, but by moving the scuttle into a major location, it meant to them the land would be preserved from their own damaging business. They also began building a wharf and fishing boats. One of the tradesmen along with the animal handlers thought it would be wise to teach them of the endless nutrition that could be found in the ocean, so along the tribespeople they began building and teaching the people how to fish.

Twenty years now passed, and the angels were getting older. Theocrites himself was beginning to feel weak. It was odd how our life cycles had functioned. These people would live into their hundreds, but Theocrites himself was already older after twenty years. Many of us found that the angels, after coming through the portal, had been given different spans in life, some of us being more youthful than others. We just figured it was luck of the draw. Theocrites was scared for his own life and began wondering if there was a way to solve this riddle.

After discussion with the locals, it was found that the more logical quarter of their first tribe moved east into the mountains. He would pursue them and find an answer with their gifts. Unfortunately, it was around that time we had found out about the demons living among us. Somehow their existence had been cloaked to us. Even the humans living in the shadows of the swamps were cloaked to us. I have witnessed people in their darkest hour, even entire civilizations bathed in darkness, but this was different. It was like the abyss claimed ownership over their lands, and we could not see through its murky shadow.

That's beside the point. So demons and angels now coexisted on one plane. Their herald, Baalthezar, had been abducted by our scouts and dragged into Theocrites' courtroom. In his courtroom, he instructed Baalthezar to get the attention of Solacrinus and lead him to the center of the plains to the south with his four choice guards. From there, they would travel east where they would find a solution to their riddle.

After their journey, Theocrites returned with his two dozen high guards and with ill tidings. The representative of Mechanus had informed them being mortal was not an abnormal fate. When crossing between dimensions, our existence would mesh with the world we resided in. Living in a mortal plane would mean that we would become mortal. Eventually, we would either die from sickness, tragedy, or age.

It was then Theocrites realized that demons living amongst them would serve to be a serious threat. If demons lived among them, the demons would use every opportunity they could to slay angels. The angels were too fragile and valuable to sacrifice, and it pained them to make such a decision, but it was then decided that they would form the Elysican Knights. They would be the first generation of half angels, trained in combat and defense. The angels would cross bloodlines with the mortals of the Bear's Paw tribe and the Stalker's Fang tribe, providing great and noble warriors.

At this time, half angels became a regular occurrence. Not all angels had been paired like Adrian and I, and when they found the opportunity of finding love as the mortals do, they married with the humans. Eventually a whole generation of half angels lived among them.

It was a good fate that the demons rarely, if ever crossed. The demons were still too absorbed with their own lands to find interest in a land of angels, and probably grew a conscience when the thought of challenging the throne would again arouse them. At least that is what we believed, for we did not know they had entered a civil war.

Theocrites was a good king, and lived a long and cherished life. He had lived for almost sixty years. During his reign, much had been accomplished and the people continued to flourish. It was also Theocrites who would meet with the representative again on the mountaintop, where he would learn of the new islands. On his return, he would have a great port built for merchant ships. Theocrites fell in love with a woman among the tribespeople who he would call his queen, and named her Jessica. From that point forward he delighted in being mortal, and for his remaining years, he would emphasize on nurturing a son who would be heir to the throne, named Virtadil.

Virtadil had been raised within the keep for most of his childhood. He spent years in the courtrooms, which had remained vacant for many years, even into his rule. At first the angels had used them for study halls so they may teach the people how to prosper with the land. Theocrites foresaw the people growing in population and would not be able to keep up with consistently educating their masses in the ways of their world. For this time, the tribespeople would be good natured but had learned to live this way over generations. Now that their lives have been completely changed, they were not sure this level of natural education would continue. The people will eventually need government, justice, and instilled virtues.

When Virtadil sat on the throne, he made a first decree, "Let it be known, from this point forward, the angels and angelic in blood will be heard in any case of conflict. Their decisions will be held paramount, for angels and their kin will be properly educated in the new system of government and justice.

"All people will now be given names. These names will provide uniqueness and lineage to define them among their people, to provide accountability and reputation in the future. They will be given a first name, for which they will be known personally, and a family name that will bear information of lineage or communal descent. In the case where further individuality is needed, middle names may be introduced. These names will also be documented during an annual census for birth and death. Those of age will have their names paired with information of trades, deeds, and mishaps.

"The purpose of this government and justice is not to punish. It is to educate, manage, and right errors. Only in extreme situations will punishment be found suitable. Those who are in position will be found to be the most gifted and wise in the terms of their position, and will represent the masses fairly. Justice will be put in place so that the wronged will be righted at the expense who had wronged. For those instances that expense cannot be found, for things of an invaluable matter, years of servitude and public awareness will be made for said actions. For those of an extreme situation, they will be removed from society for they will not be trusted until such a point that they are ready to re-enter society.

"The justice we will instate will be built on common law, and settled in Privy Court. Disputes of a form that have not been settled before will be brought forth to me, or my successors in the case that I am succeeded. There a verdict will be made, carried out and documented for future use. Any decision from that point forward will be made will be carried out and continued to be carried out as it was found in the first instance, as it was believed to be the best interest of the people and those involved.

"We will begin educating the masses of virtue and justice. Virtue will be taught to all on full scale. Even half angels will learn of virtue since they are of mortal blood and have not experienced heaven or its teachings over eons as their parents had. Virtue will teach of all the good natures of attitudes and behaviours that will allow our civilization to continue to thrive. They will not be demanded of people, we still believe in the freedom of choice. We will, however, demand a level of knowledge of these practices to prepare the people for living amongst each other. We will also teach a level of vice, for vice can tarnish and decay our people and separate brother from brother. They must be aware, not only for themselves but to aid their brothers in decision making, and for witnessing when said wrongs are being enacted so the authorities could be readily informed.

"All people will have to be aware of justice and its cause. Justice is a due process used to discern an act, its truth, the extent of the damage caused, and an appropriate method of righting the wrong. This does not mean that all forms of justice will end in punishment. For instance, theft will be dealt with by replacing what was stolen, with a personal investment in recompense. This process will aid in bringing to light the wrong, righting the wrong, and forming an apology. Under serious circumstances, these methods will become more extreme, but nonetheless, all people will have the right to due process."

For the first several decades, most of the courtrooms had become classrooms, where their youngest and newest generations would learn of virtue and justice before entering the masses. From there, they would take on trades as their parents had, or have the right to request which path they feel fit to lead. Many of the first Elysicans would become knights, and many of them would be drafted. Over time, the Elysican Knight position would be sought after, as it was found to be the most honourable of choices, pitting their very lives to preserve their way of life.

Angels continued to pass through the gates, except on much rarer occasion. Since long ago they had already concluded who would stay and who would leave, it was left to choice who would continue as a mortal. Our positions within the heavens were many, and for every one of us who left, our creator continued to populate our lands. It was joyous, but then we also realized that we would never return.

Eventually, angels passing through the gates would tell us of the fate of mortal angels. Apparently our creator, in the gift of mortality, had given us mortal soul and presence. When we died, we would no longer return as angels. We would become mortal souls and tended to by the other angels. This became a great weight for all of us to bear, knowing that we would never be angels again. It also explained why angels would second guess this gift, and why fewer were joining us. We didn't fret, for we loved our kin and would be with them once again. It was just different.

The artisans then taught the people of a refined craft that would allow them to shape the land. They would teach the people of diverting streams to provide water, even raising lands to protect them from flood. Then they taught the people how to raise entire buildings. In that process, they had raised Elysica Keep itself above the ground, and began building a large hill that it would rest on. The entirety of Elysica would eventually be able to seen from all corners of the land.

It was in Virtadil's reign that Elysica Keep continued to blossom. The market places had been moved aside and large barracks and armories had been built around it. The high guard and their descendants would continue to protect their keep, night and day. The marketplaces were built on spiralling roads leading down to the main land, with a primary transit road allowing direct access to the docks and main road for shipping. The merchant ships would then be utilized with several docks along the north and west shores to ease the burden of transporting supplies.

All the buildings had been erected in master crafted stonework and refined with metal and clay trims. The entire city reflected the light and could be seen for miles simply as a bright star that had kissed the earth. The keep would also be given the nickname 'The Ivory Tower', and had rebuilt it out of limestone and the whitest of marble.

The countryside had also flourished, to the point where the entire countryside from ocean to mountain, west to east, and ocean to Blood Plains, north to south, would be covered in livestock and farmer's fields. Little towns began to spring up as the population continued to flourish. Elysican blood became more common, and three common blood generations of mixing began.

It wasn't long until Dornarians became unsatisfied with their land, and traveled north in search of refuge among the Elysicans. Unfortunately, bearing demon's blood, the Dornarians were forsaken from the Elysican land. Every so often, their hearts would open and a Dornarian would find rest. In that rest, they would find love, and chaosbloods came into being.

Chaosbloods were easily found within the masses and dealt with swiftly. It was determined by Theocrites they would be given no quarter, as it has been declared by the official over all lands. They would be given a ship to sail to Paradigm and they would cast their children to it with use of a raft. It was saddening for Virtadil to carry out these mandates, but he understood their cause. This only increased his resolve against Dornarians living within Elysica.

In life, Virtadil had been dedicated to his work. He never found love or married. He found that he must sire a successor, and married for the sake of the people. He lived for 85 years, ruled into his old age, and had a successor who he named Serranil.

Serranil was also a half angel, for his mother was a half angel named Jestara. Jestara grew up as a descendant of a Sheep's Fleece and an artisan angel who became a textile maker. Her delicate nature would embrace the land in fine linens and embroidery unlike any other. Even the king enjoyed wearing her clothes. Many believe it was her attentiveness and diligence that attracted Virtadil.

Serranil was soft hearted, and enjoyed traveling the lands to meet with the townsfolk. He was the first king to almost completely avoid living in the keep. He took pleasure of living and finding justice amidst the townsfolk rather than having them travel the land in search of justice from the keep.

Serranil always had a scribe with him who would write his new laws for him. In their travels, they would witness much greater and rarer causes for justice than would ever be presented within the courtroom. It was disconcerting to feel the system had been manipulated, and his judges were making law for themselves, or evading law altogether.

Serranil called for a public inquiry. He would begin to amass scribes and talented children he believed to be gifted in justice but also in virtue. He would even choose children among the pure human born. They would be raised isolated from the masses, making them unbiased in their resolve. Eventually these new judges would supplant the system, and herald in a new age of truth within law. At that time, he had also formed an affairs committee that would monitor the daily verdicts and practices to approve of the claims. In this effect, the verdicts would be found twice to prove their truth.

Serranil began to grow a taste for combat, and was the first king to train among the Elysican Knights. It was then that he took on his queen, and the first influential queen of their time. Her name was Adira. She was also half blood. Her father had been one of the most recent from heaven and her mother was of the Bear's Paw. She was destined to become a high guard, and fell in love with Serranil not knowing he was king. I may have had a part in that.

Adira was a proud queen, strong and capable enough to shape her world. Mandate still claimed that it was the king's cause to form law, so she was never allowed to make verdict, nor make influence on the king's claim, not even for mercy. Adira found strength in making justice for herself. She continued with Serranil's ambition to work among the people and solved problems for herself. She would not represent the court system, but her judgement was just and she would always find a method of negotiating peace. She would also find strength against the Dornarians, who had become more violent since their exile. She was the first of the Elysicans to engage in combat against the Dornarians.

In time, Serranil and Adira would have a son, and name him Nobelan. Now, Serranil had been found of age to be forced into rule, and the population began to call for his presence. He began raising Nobelan himself, and Adira would assist whenever she was home. It was Adira that would continue presence among the people into her old age.

Adira began feeling pain for the people of the Blood Plains. Something inside of her, more than just her heart, beckoned to represent her people to them. She brought her band of knights along with her, and eventually met with the elders. At that point, the elders refused her influence. They made claim to tools and weapons provided by Mechanus. They had no need for angels. Their land would continue to stay strong and noble.

She returned to the Keep upset with their resolve. She had been given a special scroll. This scroll had been written in heaven and was dubbed "The Scroll of Pure Holies" for it was a song that would be sung across heaven by the first choir of angels. Adira returned to the Blood Plains in hopes of a second audience. This time, she would offer no aid and only present a gift as a token of peace. Their soothsayer would feel the gravity of the document and hold it for future generations. It was then the war began to break out.

Dornarian Marauders had been found toppling over caravans. Adira and her knights ran in to save the natives and slayed every last Dornarian. It made her feel horrible. The taste for blood was not her own. She then realized the horrible fate that would lie in store for them in the future. After the battle had ended, she noticed that one of the Dornarians had managed to slain one of her comrades. It wounded her so deep, that the disgusting feeling became twisted with hatred. She would find no love for her enemies to the south.

After this sorrowful event, she began to assemble hunting parties that would patrol the plains, even beyond the request of the tribespeople. They never found conflict with the tribespeople, but they did find many Dornarians. A little combat over a few caravans became a habit. They couldn't stay within the swamps. Being mortal Adira was afraid of what lied in the swamps. Whatever was brewing in there was enough to push the demons into the open. Something had to be done.

Adira then returned to the keep and informed the population of what began to brew in Dornar. A public meeting was formed. It was in this meeting the people decided to leave the fate of the swamp dwellers to their own devices and continue to utilize the Blood Plains as a filter. It had been decreed by the representative the land would be used for combat, and so the process would continue. This conclusion upset Adira. She knew the bloodshed would never end as long as they could continue to pass through the gates of hell unabated.

She would not listen to their decree, and decided to form a party of her own. She would utilize the descendants of the Stalker's Fang to infiltrate the land and see what had become of it. Her outfit was composed of ten of the most select in their regiment, trained by some of the most gifted of pure angels who have witnessed the greatest of kingdoms and their strategies, and were capable of adapting to any environment put before them. They had been cloaked in black threads weaved with dark blue plaid. Their plate armor and helmets had been lined with black sheep's wool and covered with black boiled leather that had been pressed, stretched and woven to the surface of the plates. Their weapons were coated in oils and soot which had been added to the steel's cooling water during forging.

That night, Adira would stay home with her husband, as they planned to infiltrate the night after. She felt she should have at least one more night with her son and husband. They would stay home, within the keep that night. Their servants would wait on them, and they sat for a finely prepared meal served on silver platters.

"Adira, I know what you're doing. Please don't." said Serranil.

"It has to be done. We need to know how far they have gone."

"There are things in there that do not like us. They won't just kill you, Adira. They will make an example of you." A tear rolls down Serranil's cheek.

"Serranil, I know this may turn to be a horrible fate, but our parents had seen acts like this for many millennia. It's in human nature to want to preserve our way of life and to storm through the darkness. We are also human, and this is my calling. It's my destiny."

"It's not your destiny. You're making a choice, and a rash one. Your son has not seen you in months. Nobelan. Please, tell mommy how much you miss her."

"I miss you this much!" said Nobelan, barely into is childhood. "Can we play after dinner?"

"We can do anything you want, Nobelan, anything at all."

"Yay!"

"But finish your dinner first, ok sweetie?"

"Ok, mom. I'll eat it superfast!" and Nobelan began shoveling his food into his mouth.

"Slow down, tiger. You're going to get a stomach ache."

"Yes, mom." As he slows down his forking motion, he takes every bite with eager anticipation.

Tears begin to well up in Adira's eyes. She would look into her husband's eyes, thinking it would be the last. They would then finish their meal in silence.

Nobelan and Adira would spend the rest of the evening playing with his toys, until he was too exhausted to keep his eyes open. He would sit on her lap as she sat cross legged on the floor, and she draped her arms around him as she cuddled him to sleep. She then calmly and gracefully rose to her feet and carried him to his bed, and tucked him in. She kissed him on the forehead and closed the door.

That night, Adira and Serranil had spent the night together, a night that would be filled with passion and distress, for they both knew they would never see each other again. They would lay eyes wide open all night, staring into each other's eyes to maintain a single moment of spiritual intimacy that would continue on into the timeless. Eventually the daylight would come, and they would embrace as if they were commanding time to leave them be, but time progressed nonetheless. Eventually, the chambermaids would arrive and they would have to continue on with their daily routine. Adira would slip on her ornate armour, and join the ranks in the barracks.

Her outfit had already bagged their newly forged armour and had a spare bag for Adira's. They assembled and exited the barracks, when two High Guards halted them.

"Hold, Queen Adira. We have been notified to not let you leave the lands today."

"We are not leaving the lands. We are simply carrying provisions for the townsfolk."

"What is in the bags?"

"Weapons and armour for the townsfolk. We have found several Elysicans who wish to squire with our finest. They bear the gift. We are going to test them."

"May we look inside?"

"By all means."

They lower their bags for the high guard and they sift through the finely made plates.

The High Guard asks, "These plates. Why are they not traditional knight's armour? They are dark. I can feel their darkness."

"They had been specially forged for night combat. The new trainees will serve as night guards and patrol the borders."

The High Guard shrugs, "Sounds legitimate to me. Night Guards, eh? Sounds like fun. Well, I guess you can take care then, milady. Be back before sundown. The king decrees it."

"We will."

Adira and her Stalker's Fangs traveled the plains until they reached a town bordering the Blood Plains. There, they had their squires waiting for them. Oh, it was true that Adira had been lining up squires to become border patrol, but only a half truth. You see, she had found those Elysicans suitable to replace them after they had gone. They would spend the afternoon giving them the armour they had worn themselves. Nobody would dare wear Adira's armour, for it was found to be too precious and a bad omen to replace her. They would store it for her return. The day was too hot for black armour, so the knights decided to train their armour only in their padded undergarments. The afternoon went by with rigorous training, and the knights would then spend as much time as possible recuperating with sleep. At sundown, they were served breakfast by the locals.

Then, they would don their newly forged gear. There was nothing like it. Their gear had been designed to fit so perfectly, not even the sound of foot contacting soil could be heard. Their flexibility was beyond comparison. They could barely see each other.

"Into formation!" Adira called out.

Within seconds, the ten would form two rows of five before her.

"Where we are going is almost certain death. If you are captured, they will not kill you right away. They will attempt to make an example of you. Do you understand?"

"YES, MA'AM!"

"We will run three by three. Donnal, you will stand in the rear. I know how much you like showing off your running backwards. I need you to keep watch."

"Yes ma'am. You can count on me. Try to keep up."

"As we enter the swamps, we will all face radially and keep an eye on all angles. We will fan out 5 meters apart. We will use our surroundings to our advantage. Is that understood?"

"YES, MA'AM!"

"If we must enter combat, we will warn the rest and take our targets by surprise. We will not be surprised. Is that understood?"

"YES, MA'AM!"

"Above all else, we must find the heart of their community. We must witness the extent of the damage within the swamps. Is that understood?"

"YES, MA'AM!"

"If we are overwhelmed, we will run and return to Elysica. We are not here to be heroes and we are not taking on an entire legion, we will run. We will run as fast as we can. If we get separated, we will hide within the Blood Plains until morning and regroup at this very town. Is that understood?"

"YES, MA'AM!"

"MOVE OUT!"

The Stalker's Fang marched through the blood plains with Adira taking the lead. They would see demons roaming the plains, attacking random caravans as they slept. It pained them, but they must be avoided. They must not be known. They would eventually reach the swamp. The swamp itself had a presence unlike any other, as if the darkness had possessed it. It smelled of death. It was no longer a swamp. It was a bog.

They slowly moved through the bog as they heard screeches, howls and whimpers in the distance. The trees themselves writhed and shifted in the coil. The beasts avoided all manner of life, even the Elysicans. Fortunately for them, they had not come across any demonic activity. Their travel continued unimpeded. Then, they saw it. An entire region of the swamp had been completely uprooted. The veins of rock walls that prevented the waters from flooding the great ravines below branching across the open marsh, working its way into the surrounding bog. In the center of this clearing, a massive city had been erected.

The city itself appeared to be toppled several times, and had been built over itself continuously. It was built in aggressive expansion, leaving older portions unmaintained and in the rot. Fires lit every segment of their land, and welled up from the fissures below, and the noise. The noise was unbearable. The city reeked of vice, and bled perfuse calamity like pitch doused over fresh soil. Not a single pore of life remained. This land was an effigy of death and decay.

Human eyes would not see it, but the Elysicans had vision beyond the mortal world. The darkness had been spewing from the center of the city, blanketing the night sky and coating the land. Even during the day, the light would never make it through this darkness. This darkness had an unholy nature about it. The demons had claimed the land for their own.

"They have grown too far. This must be stopped. We have no need to venture forth. Let us return."

Unfortunately it was then the Dornarians would smell love. The love Adira carried for her people and her family was so strong, it began to attract them. They began sprawling out of the fissure to see what had attracted them, and there they were, ready for the reaping.

"Stalker's Fang! Run!" cried Adira.

The Dornarians began to spill out of the fissure and chase them down. In the escape, several of the Stalker's Fangs had been clawed down. Even Adira had been captured. Only a few would escape, and they would live to tell this story to us. We would not even be able to tell this story from heaven, for the blanket of darkness had obscured our vision. Adira was lost to the darkness.

From that point forward, Adira was never seen again. Not even the demons would gloat of this conquest. The land cried for the first time, and was forced to hold a funeral with an empty coffin. Even with our intervention, the people lamented for a time. The king himself would not rule. The entire kingdom was left to silence to mourn its loss. Only a decade later, Serranil's health declined in his grief, and he passed away. He left Nobelan to rule, who had only reached finishing school. Nobelan's primary advisors would take over governing decisions as a temporary senate and the judges would continue to deliver justice.

In its silence, Nobelan's sadness turned to bitterness, and he would grow an absolute resolve for their enemies. Eventually the kingdom would recover but it would never be the same. Nobelan's education would continue and he would begin steering his knowledge towards justice and absolution. He pledged to himself, one day he would make them suffer a like fate. He would change the policy for teaching justice and virtue toward a more militant perspective, and they would begin teaching resolve and absolution. He wanted his people to know what it meant to be decisive and unbiased in their verdict, without questioning their motive. The new generation of Elysican Knights were more tempered than ever before.

When Nobelan first came into power, he had the entire kingdom draped in banners of the phoenix, even had a gold phoenix forged to crown the throne and carved into columns of pillars and accents of the limestone buildings. To Nobelan, the phoenix was a symbol of rebirth, and would give the people a sense that their culture had been reborn into a stronger era.

Nobelan refused to wear his father's armour. With a new era he would require his own suit of armour to represent a new king. He had the town's artisans carve a solid suit of white jade, trimmed it in gold and ivory. The armour itself would weigh well over a hundred pounds. Nobelan never took it off. Every day that he wore it, he felt himself grow larger. He then had great portions of the ceilings cut out and replaced with glass that would focus the light. The throne room would bathe in light and so would Nobelan. It was then he realized the light was as pure as the light of the heavens and fed his angelic side. He would become the strongest king to take up the throne.

Nobelan would monitor his own land to ensure its strength and prosperity, but also to enforce adherence to the law. He became intolerant of iniquity, negligence and deviance. Although he couldn't rewrite law, every law he would pass from that point on were much more firm on the people, and not necessarily reflecting the best interest of the people.

He also began revising the duties of the Elysican Knights. In his intolerance, he began building two armies. One would serve as a defensive line and one would serve as an offensive line. The defensive line would protect the city, its people and the townships. The offensive line would patrol the borders, coastline and even the Blood Plains. Even recalling his mother's attempt at aiding the tribespeople, he decided to carry through and make an active presence on the plains.

The angelic presence among the people became dominant. They had angel blood and were greatly gifted in their strengths and skills, but they did not carry the timeless wisdom of their parents. In a single generation, the angelic population changed from a docile, nurturing and embracing government of compassion, into a hardened, tempered and driven government of idealism. They began shaping Elysica into what they believed to be Utopia, and they did not care which virtues would have to be waivered. As his grandfather said, "the people would be taught virtue, but not expected to carry through. It would be their choice." Nobelan used this perspective on virtue to twist it into a form he could utilize to steer the people.

In the past hundred years, the population and productiveness of Elysica had grown exponentially. The entire countryside had been refined into farmland, the streams had been manipulated to provide life giving waters through the fields, and prosperity was bountiful. So bountiful, the streets would become full of residents and travelers alike.

Nobelan saw this and began a rigorous endeavour to rebuild Elysica. Its stone carvers would be brought to portions of the land where the earth was shallow and built massive quarries. The docks would be expanded to fit great merchant ships, and many other docks were then made along the north coast line. This endeavour took a while, but in the end, the quarries would ship carved limestone and even rarer marbles and granites to Elysica.

He then instructed his work force to rebuild Elysica, so its grandeur can be seen from all corners of the land. The people already saw it from all over, but apparently it was not enough. So, the labourers continued to build and expand the city to the point it could occupy the entire region under its roofs. Nobelan continued to instruct the people to build large walls that would encompass the city. I, for one, did not provide this inspiration, nor could I steer it. I saw where Nobelan was going with it, though. He was providing safe haven for all people in time of war, and building a castle keep.

When he focused on Elysica Keep, his master architects taught him of a great tool called mirrors. They showed that if a sheet of silver was polished perfectly smooth and placed against glass, it could reflect any light and image. Using mirrors, Nobelan then instructed the architect to design a series of mirrors that would reflect the light coming from the gate of heaven into the world. The architect built a massive multi-faceted prism surrounded by even more window wells. The lights of heaven could be seen from all over the land, even during the night.

After Elysica had been fortified, the labourers would continue into the countryside and reinforce all the towns and trade posts. The entire region would begin to be industrialized, capable of refining and producing beyond all measure that had already been built. Small factories would blossom where grains would be made into bread, looms would thread massive sheets of cloth to be made into textiles, even the slaughterhouses would refine the process of producing meats to be as little harmful to the beast as possible, as little wasteful to avoid producing odour and as productive as possible to feed the nation.

New armouries and many forges across the land had been built to accommodate the massive influx of recruits for the new military. Unfortunately with the excess in population, Nobelan would not be able to train them properly as knights, so those who would not be properly trained were to be trained first as soldiers, then as militia. Those who were chosen to be soldiers were found to be the more adept in combat and found full occupation. The soldiers would be provided sanctuary in the various barracks across the land. The militia would only be provided casual training and an armoury where they could withdraw supplies in times of need, and they would return to their residences. Many of the militia and soldiers would be pure human blood, and would only be utilized in dire circumstances.

Nobelan endeared the wolves after being raised with them as part of his community, but he knew that they had great power and with the right training could make a difference in the battles to come. Rather than utilizing them as a regular troop, he would have armour prepared for them and would train them for combat but would only allow them to enter battle if necessary.

It was then, Nobelan decided to start incursions. He would begin to send entire troops of soldiers across the Blood Plains. At first, the rabbles of starving Dornarians were picked off with ease. Eventually, the Dornarians caught on, and began sending raiding parties of their own. Great battles would be fought and won or lost. The battles themselves were not changing anything, only perpetuating the violence between nations.

Elysica continued to blossom as the Blood Plains continued to become torn. Nobelan's just resolve perpetuated the heat of combat, and instilled a belief in necessity into the people.

"Elysica! Your king calls for your gifted and strong! The enemy is on our doorstep. We may not be able to flush the darkness out of this land, but it grows and thrives much like have. In time, this war will come to the end. But as it stands, we must continue to fight to prevent them from growing forward. I know many of you have lost kin. This is our time where lives must be lost for the sake of all future generations."

It was also not me who put these thoughts into his mind. The heavens began to weep.

Nobelan still had no idea of the size or strength of Dornar, or of its current leadership. He recalled the meeting between Theocrites and Solacrinus, but he knew meeting on even ground would not be possible now that the war had begun.

His first attempt to witness Dornar came from the shore. Nobelan had a specially made boat designed to float in shallow water so that it could approach the shores of the inland delta without snagging on the silt beds. He prepared an outfit of Stalker's Fangs as his mother did, completely draped in plates reinforced with black leathers and plaid, wielding oil slicked swords. He also had them wear leather suits that were soaked in pitch that would allow them to enter the waters unimpeded. Unlike before, they had been given a measure of gold and gems in the case fate would favour them. Demons are an unpredictable folk, but one thing was for certain. They were all vain.

He instructed them to write graphically accurate notes and tie them to arrows, so if they were ambushed or captured they would shoot the arrows to the boat and return the messages to Elysica. They were expected to die in battle if need be, and take down as many Dornarians as they could. One of them was given a specific letter that would be shot at whatever hell-born keep they have built for themselves. The goal was to reach word to their leader.

Most of the Stalker's Fangs died in battle, but several returned. They all brought word of their enemy and the extent of their growth. Nobelan was now aware of the demonic capital of Dornar, and the spewing darkness that had come from their keep.

They also managed to deliver the letter, as they happened to dock in a portion of the city the people called Greed and bartered with the locals. Apparently hell spat out a mirrored representation of its circles and built it to promote growth in the most vile of manners. Their king was new and only twenty years into rule. He was pure demon. The demon blood among the people had been much more common. We also managed to barter scents that would disguise us among the people. The people could smell our love and light, and it repulsed them. It was contradictory to everything they stood for.

During their infiltration, they were picked off one by one. The residents of Dornar were unscrupulous, and did not attack them directly or with cause. They just became part of their malicious circle. It pained them to watch their brothers die and become food. They had to let it happen, though. Where they stood, hell would only devour each and every one of them. They must continue.

The Stalker's Fangs witnessed most of the city except for those portions found to be too threatening. Every moment within that city made them sick to their stomach. They could not take the rancid horror they faced. The demons were great but they could not find any viable threat. The demons were too busy warring amongst each other. There was little to no traffic entering or exiting the keep. It was impossible for Dornar to be sending regular waves of troops into the Blood Plains. It had to be random. They left Dornar expediently and returned to Elysica.

During their leave, Nobelan had rushed the carpenters to build a tower that would overlook the plains, and had a patrol set up to watch for an envoy from Dornar. As time passed, he would have the stone cutters reinforce the tower with bricks and palisades. Time passed, but eventually it came. King Rammathan would be ready to speak to Nobelan for the first time.

Nobelan prepared an envoy of his own. He would assemble his greatest high guards, hunters and archers. All would be wearing the finest and most ornate armours in the land. They rode on the most noble of steeds, and Nobelan had a chariot built to support a throne and canopy.

Rammathan crossed the plains on the backs of the wicked born atop a massive structure made of obsidian and twisted, scorched lumber. His armour was unlike any other, made of obsidian and wrought iron and appeared to be cursed with souls that would writhe in brutal agony amongst the enchanted fiery brimstone. He had several of his elites, standing on guard next to his envoy. Arrows had been sticking out of their flesh and nails were drove into their hands affixing their sadistic weapons to their palms.

Then, the two envoys met in the middle of the plains.

Nobelan was the first to call out, "Rammathan, let these lands be. The Blood Plains do not deserve your wickedness."

"Do you think this is my doing? Look there, noble king. Your brethren lay in the dirt as food for the vagrant and the beast, all for your petty spite against my people. Who are you to make claim to these lands?"

Nobelan responded, "This fate is not our own. You forced my hand. Your kind is not welcome among these people. They have the right to prosperity and you stand for destruction. Return to the abyss."

"Do you honestly think your commands work here? These people have called us here, just as I suppose they have to the heavens. We have just as much right on this plane as you have. I like it here. The air is so much crisper than in the pit. Do you know what it has too much of? Light. That god forsaken light can even be seen from my keep. If I could be given the moment, I would erase it from this land, but do you see me arguing? I have a demand for you. Let bygones be bygones, and leave our lands to ourselves."

"This will end one day, Rammathan. We will triumph over the darkness, and we will have our revenge."

"I knew it. I could smell it on you. I like your perfume, Nobelan. I wish to taste it someday."

"And your rabble will let the Blood Plains be. These people deserve the right to peace."

"You should know better, oh great and powerful king Nobelan. These plains have been destined for combat since well before our time. I cannot control what spills out from beyond MY city. My city is mine, after all. Those who live in the swamp test their fates against it. They live in true freedom."

"True freedom is the realization of one's self within their world and the responsibility of cause to create the effects they so desire. Freedom to chaos is fraud and only self-destruction."

"I'm a demon king. Have you ever considered chaos and self-destruction would be my cause? I enjoyed our chat, young king. Perhaps we will meet again."

And Rammathan left. Nobelan had been set off ease by the presence of Rammathan. Although he was not many years older than Nobelan, Nobelan knew that he was full demon, and that meant he was probably eons old. Nobelan also turned to return to his castle. He was surprised the king respected him enough to not attack his envoy, but embraced the concept of mutual prosperity. It was unlike what he expected of a demon. The demon had been enjoying his position as king.

Nobelan returned to his throne uneasy. He now realized this would be more difficult than he thought. Both kingdoms had flourished. Both kingdoms were prepared for war. His kingdom would be filled with righteousness and virtue, properly honed and reinforced with great provision. The demons, though, had their chaos and complete lack of need for self-preservation. They would continue to spew out of the pit and devour anything in their path. They would also more readily die.

When was the last time angels joined their ranks? And that's when it hit him. He would need angels to side with Elysica. The bloods have become too thin and with it their wisdom and strength. At first, Nobelan would attempt to cross the gates of heaven. Unfortunately for him, the gates were guarded by angels on the other side, and he was not capable of passing into heaven itself. He spent day after day pleading their case, even asking for representation. The angels would not hear him.

After talking with Nobelan over dinner, I found out the truth. Eventually a single angel exited the gates. He whispered to Nobelan.

"Nobelan, we will aid you. Know this. This situation is between me, you and the creator. I had been created and sent here for this purpose and this purpose alone."

"What are you going to do?"

"I had forged a signet ring with great powers. The angel who dons this ring will be your successor. Elysica requires angelic rule once more."

"Angelic rule? Are you saying my rule is substandard?"

"Not at all, but you'll understand why when these angels are amongst you. Several will follow in his wake."

"What do I call you?"

"Call me Eldritch. I will serve you directly in the coming days."

It was almost as if Eldritch knew we wouldn't have jumped on the opportunity to become mortal. They knew it had to be done. Even we angels have been granted choice, but this was something that called for immediate action. Now that we live among the people, we now embrace this decision. I realize my husband can't get over this fact, but he loves his new role nonetheless.

After we were pulled into the mortal world, two hundred new angels followed us. They serve among the mortals today as master craftsmen and our new High Guard. They had all been gifted with much more advanced knowledge that would allow Elysica to continue in prosperity.

It had been ten years now, and events were about to unfold.

*****

Journal Entry,

And now, I believe you are prepared for the matters at hand. Our land's story is very complex and has many facets that even the angels would see as unique, but unfortunately for us, the state of events has left our world in a very fragile state.

When I first began writing this novel, I was only aware of the world around me and those who were impacted by it, and it made me grieve and anxious. I wanted to change my world for the better, and poetic justice was my only outlet. Even then, I was blinded by the range of my own sight. Then, I met these fine people. Now that we have been immersed in truth, we know the gravity of our position. Our tales are only a footnote of what we are about to endure.

Our story has only begun. Listen now as I tell you our story, and how it all began with a simple Mayor's assistant from an island that knows only bliss and ignorance.

*****

The Blood Plains War

Chapter 1

Joseph is a regular young man, just rounding his twenty second year and still oblivious of the world beyond his own. He had always dreamed of a life of adventure, but their culture detracted his ambitions by sharing stories of its unpleasant and uncouth occupants. Every night, he would pose as if he could not sleep without another tale, and his mother would indulge his fantasies in hopes it would not lead to an exertion of will.

He awakes this morning to the kiss of light shining and a gentle breeze whispering through the open window over his bed. This would have been a pleasant rising, with the exception of his two bell alarm clock, which he immediately sweeps off his night table and onto the floor. Already in his father's house coat, he heads downstairs to the kitchen.

Joseph approaches the table and takes his seat. Rubbing his eyes, he yawns and asks, "Did I sleep in? How long? Please say it's still early. It's just a bright day. That's all. No big deal. Not like the mayor can fire me. He needs me."

His mother, Celeste, was a gentle woman passing middle age. Her flowing blonde hair had a hint of platinum, and her robes of silk and sheep's wool had begun to wear. She had been spending that critical part of their morning preparing toast and jam. Celeste sets the plate along with a glass of orange juice in front of Joseph.

He begins to devour his toast. With his mouth half full, he mutters a satisfied grunt and says, "Toast never tastes better than when you are in a rush." He then quickly washes down the toast with his orange juice and gasps for air.

"Careful son, your food isn't going anywhere and neither is the fair. You're going to do fine. Mayor Winston stopped by earlier and told me that he wants you to lead the new Monster Hunter to the stage. His name is Clint by the way." Celeste replies.

She watches as Joseph polishes the crumbs and drippings from his plate. It brings a smile to the corners of her lips, and she removes the plate from the table.

He leans back in his chair, stretches and retorts, "Monsters on Belliscia. I'd love to see the day. The entire world knows nothing happens here. If a monster came here, we wouldn't need a hunter. It would die of boredom."

Celeste corrects, "Now, now, you know our way of life is important. The last thing we need is a child missing. It's bad enough we have to rely on the Elysicans again for livestock."

As noon hour chimes from the Town Hall, Joseph is startled. He rises from his seat, turns to his mom and says, "OK mom, I'm off! I'll see you at the party." as he slides off his father's robe to reveal he had been wearing his day's clothes all night.

His mother smiles again and waves as he makes his way to the door.

Celeste looks to the ceiling, in hopes of an audience and asks, "Just keep him safe, OK?"

Joseph exits the house and begins to charge down the street.

Belliscia is a quaint town, one built of hand carved stone and lumber, chiseled and sanded into works of art and erected along undulating roadways of gravel and sand. Over fifty years, the townspeople had been diligent in their time and effort to build and maintain their town's homes. To this day it breathes the longevity of the day it had been cut from the forest, carrying the fresh scent of the living cedars throughout its corridors.

Along the way, Joseph is greeted by several of the townsfolk but it does not detract him from reaching his destination. He then finds himself within the town square where the carnival operators had begun preparations.

Many rows of chairs had been set out in the grass before a huge stage made of concrete and cobbles that had been built overnight with a series of steps had been chiseled from stone and lining the front. On either side of this stage stood dark marble statues carved into dragons, well over five feet high, detailed and contoured by the hands of a master craftsman. They held massive crystal orbs with delicate imperfections of fine metal veins weaving and intertwining as they grew radially from their core. A podium stands in the middle of the stage, with Mayor Winston and the monster hunter taking seats next to it.

"Moments away from the announcement. You are always the epitome of punctuality, aren't you Joseph?" says Mayor Winston.

"I do my best, sir. I enjoy being good at my job." replies Joseph.

"Well, that's why I keep you on the payroll. I would like to introduce to you Clint."

On cue, Clint rises from his seat to confront Joseph. He gives him a quick look over, while Joseph appears obviously intimidated. Clint gives him a smirk and extends his hand. Joseph returns in kind and shakes his hand. Clint lowers his hand, and points to a helmet resting below his chair. The helmet was white as ivory and stained by weather. It hadn't been shaped into a skull, but in fact was a skull.

"You see that? It's the head of a dragon turtle. Sure, you hear turtle. That thing was 8 feet tall with armor 6 inches thick and a head like a dragon. Can you imagine a massive snap turtle that could bite you in half? Yep. I have slayed it. That's its skull. Would you like to try it on?"

"I'll take your word for it. Besides, I wouldn't want to mess up my hair in front of all these people," Joseph licks his hand and tries to remove his cowlicks, then smiles. "Perfect! Makeup team and everything. I wouldn't want to spoil the show."

Clint smirks and recedes to his chair.

Joseph turns to face Mayor Winston and asks, "Winston, I get the whole podium deal, but what's with the dragons?"

Mayor Winston responds, "Nice touch? I got them for a bargain from some Dornarian merchants. They're always looking for a quick buck. Quick Joseph, get behind the podium. The people are beginning to gather."

The chairs began to fill with people who began peering at the hosts in anticipation.

Joseph stands behind the podium and announces, "Welcome residents of Belliscide, and thank you for participating in our town fair!" Joseph pauses for applause, "our great and wise Mayor Winston has something to announce to us today. Without further ado, may I present to you Mayor Winston."

As the crowd applauds, Joseph takes his seat and Mayor Winston takes the podium.

"As you may know, livestock have begun disappearing in the past couple of months. 3 days ago we found a carcass of one of these animals. There was nothing natural about the wounds it suffered. Even predators would be more humane." The crowd interrupts with a loud gasp, "Now, now. We have nothing to worry about. The first thing I thought of when I saw this is that if it starts getting bored of our livestock, when will it start taking a taste for residents. So, I went to the port city Belliscide, and hired a great mercenary. May I present to you the monster hunter! Clint!"

As Clint begins to rise from his chair, he slides his hand below his seat and grabs his helmet. He holds it in the air. He then wears it. The crowd cheers. He follows up a couple of flexes, removes his helmet, smiles, and takes his seat.

He continues, "Not many men around these parts like that, right ladies? But, hey, don't pester him now. I paid good tax money for him to be on the job." He pauses as the crowd laughs, "Now let the festivities begin!"

A few of the townsfolk pull their chairs aside, pick up their instruments and start playing folk music. Several of the folk begin taking their positions at the kiosks. The rest of the spectators begin meeting and greeting, and walk toward the surrounding kiosks of games and food.

As Joseph takes his steps off the stage, Winston braces his arm with reassurance, "Look. Today is our day. Try to have some fun, ok? I'm paying you for this. There will be no paperwork on this day."

Joseph stops in his tracks and replies, "I'm already having a great time. Besides, my mother will be here any moment."

Celeste approaches the platform and looks at Joseph and lays her hands on his shoulders. She then informs him, "That was a great introduction, Joseph. Now walk with me. I've been dying all morning for some of Rachel's chili."

Joseph sighs, "Yes mum. I'll just have a pickle."

That afternoon, Celeste and Joseph are walking arm in arm by the kiosks. They take a brief moment to purchase their chili and pickle from Rachel. Celeste senses Joseph's impatience, and they continue to walk once they obtain their meal.

Celeste turns to Joseph as he chews on his pickle.

"So why don't you spend more time with the women instead of your old mum, Joseph? I want grandkids one day you know. How about that Rachel? She's a pretty one."

Joseph lowers his pickle, and looks at his mother as she should be expecting his reasoning.

"She used to pick her nose and eat it in class. If I even try to imagine kissing her, all I taste is boogers. It's disgusting. Everyone here I know. They're family. It would just feel awkward carrying out a relationship with any of them. My children will be born with hunched backs or something. Besides, there has to be more to this life than this. Yes, it's great, but bliss is just not for me, mum. Do you remember when you used to tell me stories before bed, about that vast world out there?"

"I loved telling you that story. It was the only way I could get you to sleep."

Joseph's tone becomes heated. "That's because when I slept, it's all I would dream about. That's why I always sleep it. I know I'm living a fantasy, but it's more than this is to me."

Celeste tries to dull his emotion with a soft response. "You have to be careful, Joseph. What enters your heart influences what it yearns for. Filling it with empty dreams of foolishness will only make you bitter."

Joseph kicks at the road's gravel. "It's not about being bitter, it's about growing to be more. We don't do anything. We do our daily bread, we throw little parties, but the world keeps turning and we don't turn with it. It's a shame."

"Look. You're still young. You have all these hopes and dreams flowing through you, and it may hurt at first to not follow them, but you have to trust me. It's for the better." Celeste bumps into him gently.

They continue their afternoon playing the carnival's games, and eventually make their way home after the fireworks. As the night ends and after exhausting every last ounce of energy in his body, Joseph collapses on his bed.

That night, a storm erupts almost out of a moment.

Joseph remains calm asleep.

Until he hears a calling.

"Joseph, I have work for you."

"JOSEPH! WAKE UP!"

Joseph is startled awake from what he believes to be a visionless dream. The rain has been creeping into the room all night and began to drench his bed. A showering rain is hammering down on the roof and walls. Joseph's gasping breaths are nearly inaudible. He closes his window, grabs his house coat and makes his way to the front door cautiously to avoid waking his mother.

The lightning is prominent in the skies and is followed by crackling thunder that echoes between houses and down the corridors. Joseph glances around, and sees no one. He looks to the ground, pauses to think, then begins to walk in the rain toward the town hall. For such a lightning shower, Joseph seems to be oddly comforted by the rain. It has the perfect balance between warm air and cool water. He doesn't even react to the lightning. Walking toward the town hall almost leaves his mind unquestioning, as if walking to the town hall was exactly what he wanted to do.

Although he wishes it was a dream and he could go back to sleep, his body takes over and he begins to walk toward the stage, where the podium and chairs had been removed, and the orbs held by dragons are pulsating with darkness and shadow. At this point, his body becomes frigid. Without any control, he begins walking up the altar steps and stands between the dragons. A hole in the sky opens and Joseph is showered in a pillar of darkness.

Joseph rubs his eyes and squints. Off to the side, coming from a tent, a cry echoes through the Square.

The Monster Hunter cries out, "Back to the abyss with you, demon!"

"Demon?!? AHHHH!!!! WHERE?!?"

Joseph becomes frantic.

The Monster Hunter lunges onto the stage and takes a swipe at Joseph with a Bastard Sword. Joseph dodges the strike, leaps off the stage, and runs out of town as fast as his legs will allow him. For some reason, the Monster Hunter had no chance in trailing. Even though he was long out of sight, Joseph sees something like huge bat wings following directly behind him! The monster that has been feeding on the cattle must be chasing him!

Joseph decides to stop running after making his way to a small pond in the middle of the fields. As he goes for a drink, a lightning bolt skips through the sky above, allowing him to see his own reflection. Joseph has become a large demon, what appeared to be curling horns, scaled blue skin, the posture of a hardened stone mason, and what was supposed to be bat wings were growing out of his own back. He opens up in a roar to the heavens in anger and frustration, falls to his knees and begins to pout next to the pond.

As he regains his composure, he begins to think of what to do next. He sees a pillar of light, much like the pillar of shadow that had shaped him, off in the distance just south of the town.

"If this is not a coincidence, whoever is responsible may be at the second site." Joseph resolves.

After a couple hours of travel, he finally makes it to his destination.

"I know this forest. This was never here. How could it..."

He never remembered a large mausoleum made of an opalescent marble in the middle of the forest. He approaches the massive two door entrance and turns the knob. The door slides open with ease.

When Joseph steps inside, his jaw drops at the sight. The interior glows of luminescence, radiating from the same opalescent marble as the exterior. Pillars stem from floor to ceiling on all sides, and a white velvet carpet embroidered with gold and silver in patterns of dove feathers lines the main runway. At the end of the runway sits a sarcophagus guarded by 2 gigantic suits of ornate full plate armor wielding great swords. One of the suits is made of white jade, ivory, trimmed with silver and adorns a crown. The other is made from obsidian, trimmed and spiked with gold.

There is a girl sitting on the sarcophagus. She is draped in the finest of white silk capes with a combed sheep's wool stole, and has the accent of white leather armour trimmed in ivory and silver. Under her armour, she wears a draping silk blouse wrapped with a large white leather waist belt. From below the blouse, a skirt flows to her knees, and her tall boots of white leather accent her form to the toes of etched silver.

As Joseph steps towards the girl, the eyes of the guards glow red. A voice echoes through the chamber, announcing, "Come no closer. You have no place here."

He continues to step toward the girl.

The voice seems to emanate from the suits of armour.

"If you approach the angel, we will be forced to take lethal action."

The girl gasps. A glow of light surrounds her and Angel wings appear on her back. They flare out to a prestigious display then relax to her sides, resting on the sarcophagus.

He continues to step toward the girl. The guards come to life and step towards each other, standing between Joseph and the girl. They take up their arms and enter a combat stance.

"You have been warned."

The first guard sprints toward Joseph. Joseph leaps into the air, kicks the helmet off the guard to reveal it has no head. He evades a swing of its great sword. His fingers grow to claws as long as daggers. He rakes the torso of the guard from belly to neck, splitting the armor clean open. Water leaks from the shell, and the armor falls in pieces, spilling cogs and other various mechanical parts on the ground. The other guard begins to rush toward him, and just as it approaches him, Joseph lifts the blade of the fallen guard's great sword and the other guard runs into it, impaling itself on the tip of the blade. As it looks down to see what has been done, Joseph grabs its helmet and tears it off, followed by hammering down on its shoulders, knocking its arms off the torso, the force splitting the armour on the embedded blade. Water also leaves its neck and it crumbles to the ground.

The angel looks at Joseph scornfully.

"Okay, great. What were you thinking?"

She steps off her sarcophagus and muddles through the rubbish remains of the armour, and pulls two crystals from the piles. She puts them in a small satchel to her side, and lowers a portion of her blouse over it.

Joseph takes a moment to regain his composure. His hands shake at the thought of what had just taken place. Pain shoots through his forearm as his claws relax and slide back into the tips of his fingers. He feels he could bend his fingers, but his claws were much longer than their full length.

Joseph appears slightly puzzled and scrambles for words, "I'm sorry. I thought I just saved your life. Were they keeping you prisoner?"

"Keeping me prisoner? No. Those were my friends. They are knowledge constructs and were teaching me of this world."

"Wait. You're not from this world? I was wondering where this place comes from."

"This whole world is odd. One minute I'm bathing in light in all its glory and innocence, the next minute I'm being told about a savage world of pain and strife. How you even exist amazes me. So you must be one of the Dornarians, aren't you? Are you here to hurt me?"

"No! No. I'm just a guy from Belliscide. Well, I don't know what happened to me, one minute I'm taking a walk in the rain, the next minute I'm showering in darkness and getting chased away by a monster hunter. I just saw a white pillar of light and followed it here."

The angel inquires, "Well, I'm not what you would call an Elysican, or an angel for that matter either. I've been here my whole life. I guess it's a good of a time as any to see what this world is all about. At least now I have company. How did you get in anyway? The voice told me that those doors never open."

Joseph replies, "Well, I turned the knob and the door swiveled open with ease. Perhaps it is locked from the inside. Well, if you needed an escort, I have nothing better to do. I just happen to land on your doorstep and mess up your friends."

Jennifer pouts. "How about this: We'll go for audience with the Angel King Nobelan and figure out what is going on, and at the same time, you can buy some new friends for me, deal?"

"I've always wanted to see the world, deal."

Joseph stretches out his hand. The angel smiles and reacts in kind.

"I'm Jennifer."

"Hi! I'm Joseph."

"There is a slight problem though. If you haven't noticed, I'm a big demon. Not even a Dornarian, like, a BIG demon. They'll probably kill me on sight. Mayor Winston hired a monster hunter just to find something in the forest. If they think I'm it, I'm done for."

Jennifer shrugs, "Maybe we can use this to our advantage. I have an idea."

And so, Joseph and Jennifer return town. By the time they arrive, the dawn sun's light glistens through the fresh mildew and refracts faint rainbows on the wet limestone. Joseph can see his house on the perimeter of town and it seems to be in order, except for the door which he managed to leave open during the lightning shower the night before.

Jennifer stops and faces Joseph, and instructs, "Okay, you hide in the tree, I'll convince the monster hunter to come out."

Joseph points at her wings, "You may want to tuck those wings in."

Jennifer giggles and her wings turn to light and vanish.

"Maybe you should talk to my mother first. She has my money too. Just... let her know I'm okay. She'll help you get Clint. If you flare your wings out, she'll believe you. She loves angels. Her name is Celeste. See that? That's my house. She rarely goes out."

Jennifer nods, "Just wait here. Hide in a tree or something."

She heads into the town and arrives at Joseph's house. She notes the damp floor, closes the door, and taps a couple of times.

From the interior, a faint voice calls out, "Who is it?" The door swivels open.

"Oh, dear! Hello. May I help you?"

"Hello, Celeste. My name is Jennifer and I must speak with you. May I come in?"

"How do you know my name?" Celeste shivers.

"You need not to worry. I am a friend of your son, Joseph. This is actually about him. May I come in?"

"Pardon me, give me a moment."

Celeste lays a towel on the puddle and steps aside. Jennifer steps into the house. Celeste goes to the kitchen and begins shuffling with her porcelain fineries.

"Yes, you may. I'll heat up some water. Joseph never mentioned a woman before. I've never seen you before either. Are you from the main land? I heard Clint found a demon last night."

"Tea won't be necessary and I don't have much time, you may want to take a seat."

Celeste immediately takes a seat in her rocking chair and braces herself, hands clinging to the arms.

"Please don't tell me it has to do with the demon."

Celeste's eyes widen as Jennifer spreads her wings before her.

"Do not fear, Celeste. Your son found me in my home last night after misfortune found its way to him. Something happened last night and he is now a demon. Probably the demon this Monster Hunter had found. We must travel to Elysica and speak to King Nobelan, and I need your help."

"Oh, my lord! Is he alright?"

"He seems to be fine, but the primal thirst of the demon side is showing itself. We need to move. He said you had his money. Also, I need to speak to Clint. Can you come with me?"

"Give me 5 seconds and I'll gather his things." Celeste runs to the kitchen and grabs a small sack of coins from an old teapot. "There. Does he need clothes?"

"I'm afraid he won't fit in them anymore. We should hurry."

"Right."

Jennifer and Celeste head into town and approach Clint's tent. He happens to be sitting on a stool, sharpening his favourite sword. He lowers his whetstone, and wipes the blade clean with a ragged piece of dinged, suede leather.

Clint looks up to the women, and a suave yet presuming grin breaks the corner of his mouth, "Good evening ladies! Would you like to hear the story of my helmet? It's from a..."

Jennifer interrupts, "It sounds great! We need your help. You're not going to believe this, but you should come with us."

Celeste looks into Clint's eyes with despair, "Please, Clint. It has to do with Joseph."

"Anything for the common folk. Your lives are in my hands."

Jennifer takes Clint's hand and pulls him from his stool. He scrambles for his blade as his whetstone and rag land in the grass.

"You know, that was my favourite whetstone. Perfectly flat. Probably has a chip in it now."

Jennifer rolls her eyes as they march to the edge of town.

They stand before a sole tree next to the road leading into town. Joseph could be seen in its branches, but the sunrise has made a silhouette of a demon in the tree. Clint's eyes widen, but Jennifer eases him by placing her hand on his shoulder.

Jennifer whispers to Clint, "Now remember, he's a little sensitive about his condition right now. He won't hurt you."

Clint calls out, "Come out, Joseph. I'm not here to hurt you."

Joseph hops out of the tree and lands on one knee. He then stands tall. Clint is astonished.

Clint looks at Jennifer and inquires, "And he didn't try to kill you in this 'mausoleum'?"

Jennifer defends, "God no. He's harmless, except for what he did to my constructs."

"And you don't have an uncontrollable righteousness to slay him?"

"'Righteousness?' Are you serious?"

Clint shrugs, "...Just saying..."

Joseph steps towards his mother, and states delicately, "It's okay, mum. It's me. Joseph. Your son."

"Joseph!" She embraces her son.

"Are you alright? Does it... itch?"

"Mother, this is my skin. I'm fine. We just have to figure this thing out."

He then turns, "Clint, we need your help. Can you pretend I'm your prisoner and get us on a boat to Elysica?"

"We can if you don't mind being restrained. It was one of the options if what was happening wasn't caused by a beast."

"Sure. Do it. We have to move. I want this over."

"How do I know you're not completely out of your mind?"

Joseph's face turns to a pout.

"I miss my striped jammies."

Clint pats him on the back.

"Okay. You're cool."

Clint then reveals handcuffs from his belt behind him and puts them on Joseph's wrists. He attaches a long leather strap to the chain and wraps the other end around his own wrist.

"Mum, I have to go now. I will return. I promise."

Celeste says to Joseph with a shiver in her voice, "Come back the moment you get this figured out." and takes this last moment to embrace him with a foreshadowed loss. The party then walks off, leaving Celeste behind.

After a long day's travel down the gravel roads, Clint, Joseph and Jennifer arrive at Eastport. The town is very small, composed of a few shady hotels, a magistrate's office and several fishing wharfs. One primary port extends into the water and docks a single merchant vessel, engraved in detail with angelic patterns and bearing phoenix heraldry on the limp sails. The dock reeks of old fish, as it had not been properly cared for in years. The fishing vessels are all out to sea and the town appears to be nearly abandoned.

Jennifer looks at Joseph, lays a hand on his shoulder and asks him, "Joseph, can you try to hide your wings like I do? It may help us get you on the boat."

"I can try..."

Joseph releases a blood curdling roar in pain as his wings fold and pull behind his shoulder blades, and the muscles close over them. Joseph takes in a few breaths to get over the pain. Although this metamorphosis was exhausting, there had been no sign of blood among the beading sweat.

"Maybe next time we'll do that when we have to, and only when we have to."

They enter the magistrate's office. The building is small even among the sparse and simple sheds that meet the base of the wharfs. Inside the office sits a small wooden desk with a back door that appears to lead to an open storage area. Behind the desk sits a portly man, balding on the crown and face jagged with networks of well-defined creases for wrinkles. He is perfused with layers of dried sweat that stains his loose and tattered linens. A monocle hangs from his eye, and a quill is appropriately postured in his right hand. To his left sits a half spilled vial of ink which had been poorly cleaned after with wadded towels.

He positions his quill over the paper and aims for the next vacant line.

"What is your purpose here?"

"I am Clint, the Monster Hunter hired by Belliscide. I have caught their demon and am transporting him back to Elysica for formal judgment. The lady with me is Jennifer, a hired extra used to bait the demon. As payment I offered her passage to Elysica for a vacation."

Jennifer whispers to Clint, "Nice Spin."

"Papers, please. Do you have the necessary documentation?"

"Originally I felt it fit to slay the demon and move on, but this demon may be of interest to Elysica. He's intelligent, not as feral as most parasitic demons. I am bringing him in for questioning."

The magistrate lowers his quill, adjusts his monocle and reclines in his chair with his arms crossed.

"I'm sorry, young man. You cannot leave Belliscide without formal grant from a governing body. This may seem like a world where you can do what you will, but that just isn't the case. The only way you can formally transport a prisoner with demonic background is as a corpse."

Clint steps forward and presents a ruby the size of a thumb's nail, and drops it on the books.

"I know this isn't huge in the grand scheme of things, but it is a day or two off in value. When was the last time you could afford to relax? Look. We'll put him in a body bag and take care of it on the other side. What do you say?"

The magistrate's face turns red. His temper is released in a scorning tone, "Do you think I got this station by being bribed? You must have me confused with a lesser kind of person, sir. I think you should return to Belliscide and return with the necessary documentation."

Jennifer walks around the desk slowly as the magistrate keeps his eyes locked on Clint. She approaches him and kisses him on the forehead.

She then whispers to him, "Rest your mind, good sir. There is nothing but gain from this circumstance, and our reasons are ethical. If anyone decides to dig into the paperwork, they will see that there is no reason this couldn't happen."

The magistrate returns to his pale complexion and relaxes in his chair.

"Fine. Sign here."

His finger points to the line. Clint raises the quill and signs his name with an 'X' at the mark. The magistrate then proceeds to walk into the back room, and wheels out a pallet dolly. He then throws CLINT a large, black leather bag.

The magistrate stares at Joseph.

"Put this on him."

Clint pats Joseph on the shoulder and pulls the leather bag over him. Joseph then lies down on the pallet dolly. Clint finishes putting the bag around him and zips it shut. The magistrate approaches with chains ties him down to the dolly.

The magistrate then looks to Jennifer and congratulates, "Enjoy your trip. The boat will be here shortly."

They wheel the pallet dolly on to the boat and that afternoon, it sets sail for Elysica.

Chapter 2

There is Adrian, floating over the Blood Plains. The field is filled with bones of old warriors, their shattered armors and weapons, and the bones of great beasts hiding in the tall grain.

Row upon row of angels in ornate white jade armor stand vigilant.

Across from them, Row upon row of demons wearing iridescent obsidian armor stand firm.

Among the demons, a great demon with a wolf's head, giant wings and a scorpion tail foams at the mouth. It roars at the top of its lungs.

The sides begin to charge toward each other, collide with unstoppable force, and with a great flash, a sole angel with wings flared and draped in robes appears.

Bathed in light and humming a song. the world goes dark.

All he sees is his signet ring becoming visible. It is slowly spinning until its sigil faces forward.

Then, he wakes up.

Adrian is one of the last angels to step through the gates of heaven, and has now been residing in Elysica for ten years. Every year of the ten years, he had been dreaming this dream. It began when he had gotten the ring. His sweat beads from his brow and drips into his long, flowing hair, which is normally combed back and trimmed evenly to reach his shoulders. Ever since these dreams had begun, his hair had been mangled in the morning from tossing and turning all night. At least the heavens had been graceful to them. They were gifted with youthful vigor when they had entered the world and are barely approaching middle age. The tossing and turning left crow's feet below his eyes, but aging has a delicate way of reminding him of the beauty frail mortality holds.

That morning, he was lucky to leave his beautiful wife Lorelei undisturbed. He watches as the light of day illuminates her creamy skin and brings life to the subtle red tones of her auburn hair. He could sit there for hours if time would allow it, but eventually the light slowly fills the room and arouses Lorelei. She smiles as she embraces the first vision of her day, the sight of her husband entranced by her beauty.

"We have a long day ahead of us." Adrian whispers.

"I prepared our armour last night. I even had it polished." Lorelei replies.

She sprawls out of bed and opens their armour cabinet. She throws to Adrian his undergarments and padding, to which he receives swiftly and slips them on with anticipation. They spend a small portion of their morning properly preparing with each other, as donning a full suit of ornate plate is an arduous task that requires aid.

A subtle rapping on the door startles them. A messenger has arrived.

"Sorry to interrupt, my lord, my lady, but King Nobelan requires your presence in the throne room this afternoon."

Adrian shrugs and sighs, "Tell him we will be there when we are aptly prepared."

The messenger closes the door.

Lorelei opens a second cabinet, and begins laying their noble uniforms on the bed.

Adrian retorts, "I don't know why he summons us to aid in court. Our place is in the field."

"Adrian, you were an auditor for the ecumenical council of the heavens. Your place was in an office, free from conflict, and free from pain. You even had me your entire existence. I know it's great out there but you are going to be king one day."

"Who puts an enchanted signet ring in a pawn shop that decides who is to be future king of an entire civilization? Seriously. Wake up one morning, 'Hi honey', look at your breakfast, 'Ooh what's this? A ring?', 'Yes dear, I found it at a pawn shop and thought you'd like it.' Knock, knock. By the way, you're going to be a king. The portal becoming a hand and pulling me in was a real treat, too."

Lorelei plays coy, "Well, now that you put it that way, I dread the thought of buying from pawn shops. I swear I'll never do it again."

"I love you for it. Don't get me wrong. I just feel like I belong in the field with the people, not settling arguments on a throne. 10 years now and I have learned to embrace this mortal world. The fresh air, the fields, the common folk. It's living love."

"Well, that's what Kings do. Look. We can't expect the privy courts to handle everything. Sometimes they need us to make decisions too. We have to learn this. We don't know when it will be the King's time to pass."

Adrian looks to the ceiling. "Passing. Being a mortal has its quirks. Speaking of which, isn't he an Elysican too? Half human. I wonder what half is human."

"The side that understands what it means to be fragile. We'll learn great things from him. Think of it this way. Later on, we'll get to pick herbs." Lorelei holds out a few plates of her armour for Adrian to examine, "Look at my armor! I had a scribe etch patterns of herbs into it so we don't need to carry books."

"I'll enjoy examining your armor later." Adrian smirks at his wife, "Shall we?"

Lorelei blushes.

Adrian and Lorelei step through a side door that opens behind the throne and next to the gate to heaven. The throne room is wondrous and captivates all who gaze upon it. Every brick and every arch had been chiseled into perfection, accentuated with feathered scrolling and sculpted effigies of humans and angels embraced. The ceiling seems to climb for a mile, where a large mirrored prism rests directly above the gates. The entire room is flooded with brilliant light, and not a single shadow can be cast.

King Nobelan is reclined in his massive throne of gold and satins, wearing his equally massive suit of finely decorated white jade trimmed with ivory and gold as always. His four snowy white wings are fanned to his sides and rest over the arms of his throne. On his left sits a scribe on a small, cushioned chair of oak, and in front of a small desk where a book and quill rests.

The scribe stands before his chair and calls out, "All rise! Lord Adrian Arias and Lady Lorelei Arias."

Nobelan stands to his feet, and his presence is overbearing on all in the room. For a half angel, he has the stature of Seraphim, the highest order of angel knights in the heavens. His wings span his height in length, and radiate the light of the heavenly gates, "There you are, Adrian. Come sit beside me. Lorelei, it is always a pleasure to share in your company. Please."

A farmer standing before Nobelan looks to the farmer next to him and says, "We're already risen." The other farmer shrugs.

Adrian and Lorelei take their seats to his right. They are not as great as his massive throne, but they share the same fine touches that define them among men. Adrian always has trouble finding his rest, but after some shifting, he finds the spot.

Nobelan points forward indirectly at two gentleman farmers who await a verdict and mentions to Adrian, "Adrian, these two have a dispute over property. Apparently, one's goats have crossed into the other's property. He then caught them and is claiming that he owns everything on his land."

"Well, to be fair, I would let him have a goat out of the deal. He looks hungry. But honestly, that's like saying I belong to you because I sit in your courtroom. I'm not a possession. I choose to be here. Well, in a manner of speaking."

Lorelei nudges Adrian and gives him a critical glare. "I think what he means to say is that people and animal life aren't part of the property. They happen to be on them. So, the animals are trespassers. It would only be fair to let him keep one of the goats, but the man retains ownership of his livestock."

Nobelan nods to Lorelei, "Thank you Lorelei for the clarification."

Nobelan then announces, "So be it. Herdsman Jared, you may have your livestock back excluding one goat of your choice. The Angel Knights will escort you and assist with this transition. Herdsman Oleg, you may keep a goat, but you must make the rest of the livestock readily available for their return."

The herdsman respond, "Thank you, my liege." And make their exit. The scribe begins noting the verdict, and turns the page.

The door closes. A few moments later, the door reopens, and Clint, Jennifer and Joseph step inside. Joseph is still wearing chains.

Nobelan stands appalled. "DEMON!?! Why does this filth stand in my halls! Its very presence is staling my air."

Jennifer flares out her wings and steps forward with assurance, "My King, please, Do not raise your temper. He was a mere human. Some unearthly event made him this way. Watch."

Clint removes his shackles and nudges him, "Quick Joseph, convince him you're just a boy."

Thinking of the long boat trip and persecution assists Joseph, as his eyes begin to glaze over. He looks into Nobelan's and his heart softens as he says, "I miss my striped jammies."

"Jammies?" Nobelan releases a guffaw, "You mean pajamas. My lord, he's just a boy. Tell me, son, what happened?""

"I'm just a mayor's assistant from Belliscide. I went for a walk in the rain and was drawn to this creepy platform he built for a town fair. I was hit by a beam of darkness, and now I'm this. Thank God for these two. I'd probably be dead by now, probably by the hands of one of them."

Clint whispers, "No hard feelings."

"Well, I have to say, this is peculiar. Care to share any thoughts, Adrian?"

"Lorelei and I were going to visit Moranda to gather herbs for the apothecary. She could probably run some tests. We'll take them with us."

Nobelan relaxes back in his chair. He rolls his eyes and smiles. "So, you found an exit. I understand. Fair enough. Is this what you'd like, Lorelei?"

"I'd love to keep you company, this throne room is always a treat, but duty calls."

"How gracious of you. You two may have your leave." Nobelan reaches into a pocket and pulls out a sack of coins, "Here's a small purse to pick up some provisions with. It looks like these three haven't eaten in a while. Treat them to lunch, will you?"

Joseph lights up and responds to his favour, "A thousand thank you my king. We are famished. I'm still not used to this massive form. I'm actually looking forward to seeing how much I could eat right now."

Nobelan rests his hands on his belt, "The pleasure is mine. We appreciate our noble neighbours from Belliscide."

The three look to each other, then synchronize their response, "Thank you, my liege."

Adrian then approaches the three, and whispers to them, "Wait outside. We're going to gear up."

Joseph looks at him and asks, "Are you an angel?"

"The real deal, bud."

"My day is made."

Joseph, Clint and Jennifer wait patiently on the steps to the keep's courthouse. The wait goes on for a short while. The courthouse itself is surrounded by several large buildings, most of which appear to serve a military purpose. Many soldiers march in formation, the stables are active with shoeing and combing, and the skies are filled with angels soaring around the keep's ivory tower.

Eventually, Clint takes his stand. "It's been real, folks, but I really need to go my separate way. Maybe we'll bump into each other again sometime."

Jennifer appears distraught, "But we just got here. Are you sure?"

"Look. It makes me feel good that I gave you a hand, but this whole traveling thing? They're going to see Moranda. She's a fabled witch in the Dornarian swamps. I can't go back there. I'm sorry."

Jennifer hugs Clint, "Fair is fair. We'll miss you."

"Helping us really means a lot to me. Stop by Belliscide sometime. Maybe I'll be human again by then." Joseph says.

"I'm from Eastport. It'll probably be sooner than you think."

As Clint walks away, Adrian and Lorelei step out from the court hall.

Adrian looks to Jennifer and Joseph, "Where's he going?"

Jennifer replies, "He needs to do his thing."

"Awkward... okay." Adrian claps, "Who's up for some grub?"

Lorelei holds Jennifer's hands, "And we must do some shopping before we go."

Adrian says, "We'll hit up the marketplace. I know a great place there and it's right by our favorite shops. They have everything."

Jennifer's eyes light up, "Sounds great!"

Joseph nudges Adrian, "I hope you have a big wallet."

"The biggest."

Walking toward the marketplace, the townsfolk begin to eye Joseph. Very few of them had ever seen a demon before, and even then are not poised to welcome one. The tension begins to sadden Joseph, but they continue on their walk. Even the guards are keeping a close eye on him. Even with Adrian and Lorelei by his side.

Adrian attempts to comfort Joseph, "Don't worry about them. They love you. They just don't know it yet. Give it time. You're one of us now."

As they approach the marketplace, Lorelei takes Jennifer by the hand and they run off into the shops. Adrian and Joseph are left to wander the corridor.

The marketplace houses a multitude of limestone and sandstone shops at a range of heights and stand side by side with tents at their storefront selling a variety of goods and services, ones of the like would have never been introduced to Draemoria without the aid of the angels. The streets bustle with activity, people from all walks of life buying from the shops and trading with each other. The corridor itself is very wide, capable of supporting plenty of people, but also oxen carts and carriages. Children play in the streets unsupervised, and live carefree. Several of the children, travelers and shop owners don angel wings, but very few have the same presence of Adrian and Lorelei. Joseph also witnesses wolves wrestling and rolling with the children.

Adrian says to Joseph, "You know what the best part of being an angel is? Living for so long, experiencing so many different civilizations, and seeing the good in them, especially when we apply those memories to our restaurants."

At that moment, they begin walking through the dining portion of the marketplace. The aromas fill the corridor and coalesce into one symphony of delicacy.

"Everything here is so wondrous, and smells delicious. I just want to try everything."

"The key is to not allow it to overwhelm you. There are so many flavours here, and you may try them in time, but you have to start by choosing one. Try to focus on just one aroma. Don't let the strong ones cloud your judgement. Look for the one that calls to you."

Joseph takes a moment to release the air from his lungs, and slowly inhales to smell every last scent that passes through his nose.

"I smell it. It smells, like herbs. Delicate herbs, not even roasted. They are just breathing their scents into the air."

"That's the salad, and that's just the appetizer. That's where we'll eat."

"Living on Belliscide was supposed to be bliss. I guess they had a twisted view of what bliss was. More like a cage. Do you have any idea how long I've been dreaming of seeing the world?"

"I have a feeling you'll be seeing it all. Life is like a flood gate. Open the gates, and it rushes over you. Sometimes even more than you can handle, and I'm telling you now, I didn't choose to be mortal, but it's worth it. So, do you have a thing for Jennifer? You seem to be warming up to each other."

"Well, I'm a demon. A BIG demon. I think I intimidate her."

"Do you see how she looks at you? I know she's not an angel. I know it. It's part of me and who I am, and that is not an angel. She's just like you, trapped inside a form not meant for her. I think she can see right through you because she's going through the same thing, even if she's not willing to say it. Persevere, my friend. Persevere."

Jennifer and Lorelei approach with hands full of shopping bags, illuminated by the day's ventures. Jennifer hands Joseph a suit made of leathers, deep blue linens and fashioned with metal plating.

She begins to show him the details of the suit, "I know this isn't your jammies, but it will look good on you. It will keep you safe. See? It's got metal plates on it. And it'll make you look dashing. Like a knight in shining armor."

Adrian pulls Joseph close with an arm around his shoulders, "Knight and shining armor right here. Now this makes two of us, right?"

Joseph smiles, "It can't get any better."

Lorelei asks, "So, have you boys decided where we'll eat?"

Adrian replies, "Joseph here has picked out 'The Flower's Petal'. They have great tea there."

Lorelei is enchanted by the thought, "Oh how I love that restaurant. Fill up on herbs, go gathering for more. Sounds like a plan."

They begin walking toward the restaurant and are seated on the patio. They spend the afternoon laughing over the simple moments in life and enjoying the delicacies their purveyor has to offer. At the end of the meal, Joseph leans back in his chair as he had never been this full in his life. The waiter approaches the table, and Adrian hands him a small sack of coin. The waiter weighs the sack and smiles as he walks away.

The party then walks out of the marketplace and follow the wide corridor to the gates of the city.

Joseph asks, "Are you sure we don't need anything? Not even pots?"

Adrian responds, "Don't worry. We're trained survivalists. We can spend weeks out in the field. Trust me. You're going to love this next bit."

Without amassing provisions necessary for a long and arduous journey, they begin to march towards the Blood Plains. The Border to the Blood Plains could not have been more defined. After spending a few hours crossing farmer's fields and waving at their neighbours on their way, they get to a point where the combed and nurtured fields of grain cease and wild, tall grasses begin. This seam carries on as far as the eye can see, from shore to mountain. Adrian draws his sword and pulls his shield off his back. Lorelei readies her bow in one hand and pulls an arrow from her quiver with the other. Although they have their weapons at the ready, they appear relaxed as they continue to march on.

As they begin to walk through the tall grain, several tribesmen of the Blood Plains ride forward on horses, bareback. Their clothes are a combination of painted leathers and green linens, and their faces smudged with pigments representing their tribe as the Horse's Mane.

The leading tribesman calls out, "Your kind has no place on our land. Present yourself. What is your business?"

"I am Lord Adrian Arias, future king of Elysica, this is my wife, Lady Lorelei Arias, and these two are Joseph and Jennifer, our friends. We're on a diplomatic mission to the Dornarian Swamps."

"What would a future leader of a civilization want from gallivanting around in his enemy's land? Or is he just looking to satisfy his desire."

"Unlike some Elysicans, I have no need or desire for worldly temptation. I am a pure blooded angel. We are gathering resources that can only be found in the swamps for our apothecary."

"So you mean to see Moranda. I'm sure you will bump into a few of our associates on your way. Carry on."

As they continue to march on, Adrian turns to the rest, "So official and stiff for tribal plainsmen aren't they?"

In the distance, the spokesman can be heard, saying "We heard that. We're not stiff. We're on duty."

Adrian remarks, "Stiff."

The rest of their day continues on unimpeded. Adrian explains to the rest that the people of the Blood Plains avoid contact because of the years of tragedy that befell them. As they walk through the tall grass, they move into patches of bare earth that had been trampled by soldiers and beasts alike, their sundered equipment and bones still riddling the plains. Every so often, these bodies are more recent, being dead for only days. Some scenes have to be avoided as they carry the scent of decay on the wind.

Yet again, they reach a defining line between the lands. The tall grass ends abruptly and becomes tangled in the thorns and overgrowth of the Dornarian Swamps. The swamp is perfuse with strange odours and hangs with an eerie and ominous darkness, one beyond the shade created by the thick canopy of treetops above.

Adrian begins to step into the overgrowth, and waves the rest forward, "Stay close. This can get dangerous."

Chapter 3

And here we are, sitting on the steps of a town hall, a quiet and sundered town living among the filth of its depressing depravity. We had taken up minutes from the town hall, where it had been reported one of their maidens had been snatched away from town the night before. This is a common occurrence in the swamp, either from temptation or picking the prime of the herd to barter within Dornar itself.

As we sing her song and play our instruments, my heart begins to hang low.

I lower my lute, turn to Syrenne and say to her, "Tragic. A fair maiden, once a light amidst the dark simply vanishes into the dark, and the dark pays no mind, as it's satisfied by the dark. Do you think they will miss her?"

Syrenne then sighs and replies, "Unfortunately the only one the darkness misses is itself. A strange fate to be in the one place where light would be extinguished with joy."

"Well? Shall we?"

"I see no harm."

We proceed to leave the village and search the swamps for this lost maiden, in hopes we could rescue her before what fate may have in store for her. For all we know, she may have been carried off to Dornar. It is not our position to assume the worst. We always do our best to do what we can.

Unfortunately, our best is not soon enough. The maiden lay cold and still on the ground, with fresh mud on her flowing, sky blue gown. Kneeling over her is an oafish half demon Dornarian, searching for body for valuables.

My disgust overwhelms me and my newfound persona takes hold, announcing to the demon, "Oh, how you must feel so privileged to get away with murder in the one land where you would not be punished. With a brain that small and a skull so thick you probably would have met your fate long ago. I guess even swamp scum finds its recesses in the depths of the most undesirable holes of effluence."

The demon slowly rotates its head to face us, black drool hanging from its mandible, spitting a guttural and loose interpretation of the common tongue, "Oh, come now, bard. Savoring such a morsel of innocence is twice the kill of anything else in this swamp. Let me enjoy my feast in peace. These are our lands."

Syrenne is trying to keep her composure, but can't help but join the conversation, "Perhaps you wouldn't be hungering for souls if you had one yourself."

"So the bird has a voice of her own, too. I wonder how it sounds with shrilling screams."

I draw my scimitar and point it at the beast, "Enough of this. You'll taste your fate brewed with a dose of justice."

The Dornarian reels around on his knee and leaps onto his feet, as he begins to charge, Benneth takes his opportunity. He leaps out of the shadows, cleaves a cross section out of what was once its neck and sends the neck meat disc soaring through the air. As its head tumbles to the ground, Benneth uses the momentum of its falling body as a wall to kick off of, and lands on the branch of an overhanging tree.

I looked at him with spite. At this time, I had only been friends with Benneth for a couple of weeks and my heart was still hardened with violence.

"That was my kill, and you stole it."

"I stole nothing, and you should not be relishing in murder." He then proceeds to shake his finger at me and looks at Syrenne, "Can you believe this?"

Although I am wearing my mask at that moment, I can feel my face heating and turning red. I then scorn Benneth, "What is poetic justice without the justice? I must have my justice. I feel like an unfinished symphony perpetuated by a heartbeat and nothing else."

Benneth consoles, "Aww. Try not to be so cynical. It pulls away from your character."

"Pulls away?... Now we can't have that, can we? Perhaps we should put a new spin on this ballad." I then glare at Benneth, "Death comes for us all, like a thief in the night."

And that is when Adrian, Lorelei, Joseph and Jennifer entered our lives. They must have been standing there for a while and appeared amused by our display.

"Oh. Hello! I didn't realize that Elysicans travel this far from home. This land takes light away, and the light shines ever brighter in return. A joyous occasion!"

Benneth pipes up, "They're not putting on a show. Believe me. This is how they actually talk."

I return to scorning Benneth, "Listen here, death thief. Life is poetry. When you understand its poetry you may understand what it means to live. No wonder it perplexes you so..." I then look toward our acquaintants, "How long have you been standing here for?"

Adrian replies, "Long enough. What's with the mask?"

"Oh, a thousand pardons. May I introduce myself." I remove my mask, "I am Sorrownote, of the Minstrels of Murder. We travel from town to town sharing news for the illiterate. On the side, we strive to be the hands of poetic justice in this god absent and unpleasant bog."

Syrenne then reminds me, "It's an inland delta, honey."

"And I'm Syrenne, his life partner and harpist. We've been traveling in and out of here for some time now. Have you?"

Jennifer steps forward to Syrenne, "Actually this is our first time here. We're following Adrian and Lorelei to visit Moranda the witch."

Lorelei inquires, "I take it you are from the Blood Plains?"

I respond, "Yes, yes we are. We wear costumes so the darker side of this bog doesn't see us for our humanity. It gives us an edge. I like feeling edgy."

Benneth then interrupts, "I'm not one of them. We happen to meet a few days back. I'm a chaosblood Probably the purest of us. I have no human blood whatsoever."

Joseph is intrigued. "A chaosblood? But aren't you supposed to be banished to paradigm?"

"Well I was. I was taken in by one of the oldest of us. He was eaten by a predator. I killed that predator and took his gear. Then I slowly gathered bones and skins from my prey to make a boat and after a long and arduous journey across the ocean I made it here to Dornar. Would you like to see my boat?"

Lorelei shivers and steps between them, "Umm... creepy. Let's not."

"You can call me Benneth."

Syrenne then asks, "So you're looking for Moranda, is that right? You know that she constantly travels. Do you know the secret word?"

Lorelei replies, "Actually we've been notified that we would probably run into you by some of the border guards on the Elysica side of the Plains. Thank God we did."

"That's fine. We'll take care of you. We've been watching her lately just to keep her safe. Could you imagine what demons would do to her if they found her?"

Jennifer is then overcome by remorse as she see sees the maiden in the mud.

"Something like that?"

"With a witch as powerful as Moranda? No. They would either turn her, sacrifice her, or throw her into the bowels of the abyss as a finger puppet."

Jennifer then recalls the teachings, "I didn't realize their portal is so powerful."

That's when I explain, "Well, angels don't have much of a reason to come through to our plane, and they are long lived when they do. Plus, the big guy upstairs rarely lets anyone from this plane directly into heaven. He appreciates life so much he wants us to live it out. The problem with demons is that they have such a high turnover rate. They love coming up and being mortal to sate their desires, which often leads to sending others back to the abyss just to crawl out again. It's a pity when a human gets 'taken' by these things. Their souls become so lost. Then you get abominations like this one." That's when I begin to kick at the torso of the once living Dornarian.

Benneth then interrupts again, "He has no appreciation for those 'things'."

"Your mother was one of those 'things'."

That's when Benneth takes his opportunity to correct me, "Actually my mother was a herdswoman from Elysica. My father was the half-demon, and half-human who fell in love with my mother."

And I try then to compose the poetry to his existence in this world, "I will need to grasp this. Wait. Even in the darkest corners of the land, love and life can still be found, even if buried in the darkness. Light calls to light, and although is impeded, refuses to falter. You see? Your existence is poetry."

Benneth finally appreciates my skill. "Thank you."

Syrenne then glares at everyone until she obtains all of our attention, "So, first we bury the victim, bury the half-demon upside down and dump a vial of acid on his body, then move on. Sounds like a plan?"

I then continue, "The more melancholy portion of the poem. Oh how I loathe the cleanup. So depressing. Unfortunately we can't even prepare a eulogy for this one."

Syrenne embraces me, "We'll save the next one. They can't win them all."

Benneth points at the mudded and perfuse waters, "We are in a bog, Perhaps we can just slip them in. No offense."

Adrian sides with Benneth, "We're not prepared for this anyway. This is just, upsetting. We should probably use stones to weigh them down. The last thing we need is our presence felt."

"I know you're pure blood, angel. I can smell you. Demons will start smelling you any time now."

At that moment, golden eyes appear in the darkness of the thick canopy. Several demons had been hawking over them, entertained by the events that had taken place. Their silhouettes had been unmasked by their now gaping maws, bearing teeth white as ivory and dripping with saliva. The stench of death escapes their bowels on their breath and hangs over the stench of the bog. Their claws dig deep into the branches as they leap down to strike their newly found prey.

In quick response, we all turn our backs to each other and raise our weapons. The demons begin to gnash at us, but they are no match for our puissant skill at arms. Benneth is amused by their efforts and begins moving in and out of the shadow, separating limb from body. I managed to fell my opponent before he had been given the opportunity, and I utilize the moment to deliver a quirky grin.

Even though we had vanquished our assailants, we leave the battle battered and bruised. Lesions begin to drip blood. Even the angels had been marked by death.

Jennifer begins to approach each of us, and her hands radiate with light. She then heals us, leaving not a mark on our bodies. Even Adrian and Lorelei are shocked by her gift. Not even angels can heal like this.

Benneth asks Jennifer, "What are you?"

"I don't know."

That's when I take note of our scene, littered with dismembered demons and our previously fell victims. "Don't worry about burying. We have to leave this now. There is no time. They'll even feed on their own like carrion."

I then show our new companions the way to Moranda's Hut, swiftly before our scents linger.

Syrenne and I are standing at the lead when we arrive at an open bog without a canopy. This spot appears to be the only spot without a canopy for miles, and yet the hovering darkness persists, preventing the daylight to pour through with its refreshing sustenance. Not even the open wound allows fresh air to enter, and remains thick with the effluence of the bog.

I then call out, "Reveal yourself, Moranda!"

Adrian turns to me shocked, "That's the secret word?"

I responded, "I never said it was clever."

My companions look around as if something was supposed to happen.

Jennifer remarks, "It's just more bog."

I look at her and ease her with hand gestures, "Wait for it."

The bog dissipates to reveal a hemisphere of fresh air, surrounded with a shrub line and moat at its circumference. A short footpath of cobbles and gravel leads to a gated entrance. As we enter, we behold a pleasant yard. The center of this yard holds small garden encompassing the base of a tree with a crystal clear pond that has river stones for a bed, and a hut that appears to be made of stitched sheets of leather and has a stone chimney protruding from the rear. Even the sky is bright as day, breaking the bearing darkness with its presence.

Jennifer is exhilarated by the site and exclaims, "How beautiful! She must spend hours tending to it."

Lorelei says, "You'd be surprised. Her entire yard is magical up to the moat. Can you believe she can turn it all into a marble?"

"Amazing!"

Moranda then steps out of her hut to greet us, "What a perfect afternoon. So many guests! Come in! Come in!"

"It would be a pleasure." I reply

"We'll be fine in the garden, if you don't mind." Lorelei says.

"You two go ahead. I realize you're probably on an errand." Moranda says, "As for you two, I've been expecting you." She points to Jennifer and Joseph.

Lorelei and Adrian make their way toward the garden tree as the rest of us go into Moranda's hut.

As we step inside, Syrenne and I take a seat on her sofa. I begin playing a ballad on my lute as Syrenne hums along. She then reveals her handheld harp and begins plucking notes. Benneth overlooks us from a corner of the room.

Moranda points at her dining table, "What a treat. Joseph, Jennifer, please sit at the table. Let me gather my things."

She then stands before her alchemists' table and begins assembling a rack of vials. She sits between Joseph and Jennifer, and stares at Joseph.

"Now, Joseph, some of these may be discomforting. First we must discover the nature of this curse."

Moranda reaches for the first vial and pours it in his tea cup. With a slight bubble, a hand of water rises out of the water, as if clutching for air, then returns to the cup. Joseph gasps and glares at Moranda.

Moranda begins mumbling to herself, as if she is insulted by his reaction, "I assure you, this is not poison. Like it would matter in your new form anyway..."

Joseph drinks the whole cup in one tilt of his head. He begins to gasp for air as he appears to be choking, but then stops.

He lets out a guffaw. "You should have seen your faces!" and begins pointing at everyone. As he points around, he notices his hand shimmering with human skin, but it turns demonic in a moment.

Moranda explains, "Well, that was the first test, Joseph. That magic was an anti-magic elixir. The only problem here is this is the highest dosage I can give you without killing you. At least we know that it is a conjured transformation, and not a metamorphosis."

Moranda pours Joseph another cup of tea, and begins pouring in the second vial. The glass rumbles a bit then returns to normal. Joseph drinks it down, and out of his mouth and eyes shoot rays of light.

Joseph grabs his stomach with both hands, "AH! My insides! They burn!" With one belch, he is satisfied.

The second test was a vial of Pure Light, harvested from plants I have positioned to grow in the light casted by Elysica's tower. My intention of this spell was to test the polarity of the curse. Although you have taken a demon's form, I had to prove the nature of the magic. It appears that it is in fact a concentration of darkness in your body that has given you this form, as Jennifer has been made angel from hers. Yes, Jennifer, the form you take on is also unnatural. I can sense a commonality between you two."

"Well, next time I decide to have a 'Pull My Finger' joke at a reunion, I know who to ask." Joseph exclaims.

Moranda grumbles as she leans toward the third vial. This vial, she picks up with both hands, and hands it to Joseph directly. When he takes it from her, he notes its weight and grabs it with both hands before it drops. When he drinks it, his stomach sinks. His face shimmers with stone.

"I feel stiff. What is this?"

"Don't fear, Joseph. I'm testing a simple petrification potion. I wanted to test your immunity for more natural spells and curses. Some creatures of your form are resistant, others are immune. I am afraid I can do nothing for you, but do not fear. There is a cure for you out there, and you will stumble upon it when the time comes, that I can assure you. Ok, everyone! We can go back to the garden now. Something concerns me and you all must hear this."

Moranda rises from her seat and exits the hut. The rest follow en suite.

Adrian and Lorelei happen to be lying in the tree's branches, picking herbs. They examine her armor for specific herbs etched into the plates. They take a moment to meditate on the chosen herb, and with a smile, the herb blossoms. They then pick the herbs and put them in a large pouch with multiple pockets. In that moment, Adrian had just picked a growing herb and fed it to Lorelei.

Moranda clears her throat.

"That's enough picking, you two. I must speak with you. Have you seen odd packs of demons traveling together lately?"

Adrian turns to face Moranda.

"Actually, we were just forced to slay one before we trekked over. What's the problem?"

"Those aren't just regular packs. I've heard rumours that King Rammathan is planning to attack Elysica on their own soil without provocation. Something has his heart in a knot. More than usual, like he's spitting acid."

Lorelei spins around in fear, "Elysica! This is horrible! So many would fall victim to the demons before the angels could respond. We must go home and warn King Nobelan immediately."

"For some reason I had a feeling you'd say that." Adrian begins to ponder. "Hold on. But how do we deal with King Rammathan?"

Benneth steps forward. "Leave him to me and the big demon here. You go ahead to Elysica. I bet 'his highness' would not appreciate seeing my kind there."

Joseph looks at Benneth, "Do I get a say in this? Demon capital city it is. I guess…"

Jennifer crosses her arms and holds herself tight. "I feel so exposed."

I then comfort her by saying, "Maybe you should come with us to the Blood Plains tribal council. We could use a hand there. We'll try and convince them to settle this conflict."

"Shouldn't I go back to Elysica?"

Lorelei says, "It's probably best you go with them. I think the King doesn't know how to take this situation in, and we have to speak in a more private setting about this. Go with Sorrownote and Syrenne. They'll keep you safe."

Jennifer stares into Joseph's eyes for a last moment and says to him, "Be careful."

"I will."

Adrian then says to Moranda, "Moranda, it's always fun. We really must be leaving."

"It's understandable. I knew this was going to happen, too."

"How do you always do that?"

"Just call it 'intuition'."

"Gotcha."

As everyone has a last moment together, embracing and assuring, Adrian informs us, "Whether this goes sour or not, we should all meet at the Blood Plains in the middle."

I add, "Around the center of the Plains is a field riddled with broken equipment and bones. They usually fight there since it's one of the most travelled paths. Joseph, Benneth, you can't miss it. Demons aren't that clever. They'll probably use the same route if they decide to attack, and even then, it's very well trampled from the past."

Benneth responds, "Will do. We should only need 3 days' time. That includes travel. If I can't stop the King, I will end him."

Joseph is not impressed and looks over Benneth, "Wow. Big speak for a little guy. I heard the demon king is huge. Like HUGE."

"I'm... special. I'll tell you later. Either way, Adrian, get your soldiers out. If they hit, they'll hit hard. If they don't, at least you'll have a nice parade."

Lorelei says, "I hope this doesn't get messy."

Syrenne says, "I'm sure it won't."

As they begin to leave, Moranda pulls Benneth aside and slips a vial into his gauntlet.

Moranda whispers to him, "Be careful with it. It's Liquid Reason."

As they leave her yard, Moranda and her haven disappear into the night.

Chapter 4

Dornar is a fallen city, perfuse with sin and vice in its rawest, most vile form. Even those who would enjoy vice are disgusted by the sight. Humans would perceive it as the realization and culmination of all children's nightmares.

Imagine a land so twisted, even if there was pleasure to be found, pain would find its way first. The city itself is contorted by ages of layered destruction and rebuild, and even from the edge of the clearing can be seen as segmented, for each segment focuses on a different perspective of culture within the abyss itself. Veins of paired brick walls run randomly from its center, and peering down between them reveals miles of excavated, demon made fissures with a series of tunnels penetrating its walls. Demons and half-demons circulate the carved corridors and tunnels, clawing at the walls with their bare hands and hauling brick and ore in carts. The city glows with fire and brimstone, and shrill screams and maniacal cackles resonate from all corners and below.

Joseph and Benneth remain hidden within the bog, overlooking an entranceway.

Benneth looks at Joseph and says, "Think of me as your guardian angel."

Joseph responds, "How so?"

"Well, something about being pure demon and angel blood. I can walk through shadows."

"Through shadows? Right."

"Watch."

Benneth slips his hand through a dark side of a tree then pulls it out. He then looks at Joseph and smiles. Joseph stands dumbfounded. He then steps into the shadow and disappears.

"Ok. Nice trick. Come on now. I'm scared here."

Benneth exits the shadow, "Don't be scared. Whatever you do, don't be scared. You must be a demon right now. Get into it. I'm going to find a safe junction in town for you. I'll be watching you on your way in. If you're threatened, I'll.... take care of it. Ok?"

"Yeah, Ok. I'm a demon." Joseph attempts to look scary, "Grr…"

Benneth pats Joseph with a quick, single pat on the back, "That's the spirit!" He then re-enters the shadow.

Benneth himself is dumbfounded. The scenery has changed substantially. At first, wandering through the bog, everything just felt like rot. This scene before him is completely different. Animals are left to rot, and the city still feels alive with presence. Benneth had never felt the presence of other beings within the shadows before. Dornar itself still stands, but appears to have crumbled and eroded from eons of wear. He is surrounded with a stench of death, much more perfuse than the bog before.

"Death? What is this?"

He begins to walk through the vacant Capital City. As he walks through, he still bears witness to the vice and calamity filling the streets, although the world is much slower, as if they had been caught in a thick fluid and even their speech sounds muffled and slowed. The portion he must be walking through is associated to anger, but all forms of wickedness fill its streets. The sight makes him nauseous, and he focuses on the road ahead.

For the first time ever, Benneth sees beings living in the shadows. They have no faces, only eyes.

As he walks through the crowds, he notices that they are starved and riddled with plague marks, but they are more like scars than lesions. They pay no attention to him, as if they are adrift with no cause.

Benneth calls out on the top of his lungs, "What the hell is going on here? Can anyone speak? Hello?"

Not a single reaction or a change in the spectre's drifting paths.

But then, in the distance and in the fog, six spectres emerge and begin to walk toward him.

One of the spectres, with a voice much like a winded Syrenne, begins to resonate, "Hello, Benneth. You are Benneth, aren't you?"

"Who are you? What's the matter with these people? Wait a second. What are people even doing here?" He begins to wave his arms in a random stray's face, and it stares vacantly without a blink.

A second spectre begins to speak, one with a voice similar to Jennifer, "We don't know who you are or who we are, really. We do know you, though. We were told you would be here at this very spot."

"Ok, now you're freaking me out. How do you know me? Where am I?"

The third spectre, sounding like Adrian says, "What we do know is that we're standing at the end of the world, as it dies, and we are left to drift here. We were told you would be here. You need this"

The spectre hands Benneth a rolled up piece of parchment.

"What the hell. Can you please just lay it straight? What is this?" Benneth begins to unroll the parchment.

The fourth spectre, sounding like me stops Benneth immediately and explains, "No! Gentle! That is the only one and it must remain that way. That is the last page in the book of this world's life. We were told to give it to you."

"The end of the world, eh? Then why is it just here? Why isn't it the end of the world anywhere else?"

The fifth spectre, sounding like Lorelei then explains, "You must understand. You will know yourself soon enough. You must know this. The world is ending. That page is only days old. If you don't fix this, we will all perish."

"But this is the end of the world, and you're already dead. Why should I care?"

The sixth spectre, sounding like Joseph says, "Because you care enough to stop a war. This war will be the death of us all. Read the scroll."

Benneth begins to read the scroll.

"No. This isn't right."

He rushes back to meet with Joseph.

Joseph is patiently waiting outside the gates of Dornar, when two half-demons, whipped and tormented as a slave and bulging from years of slavery sprawl out of a brick vein. Their contorted forms are accentuated with wolf's maws, and they adorn horns of an oxen. They confront Joseph and begin circling him as they examine him.

The first half-demon says, "Fresh out of the pit, are we?"

The second half-demon says, "Certainly smells fresh. Not even a hint of brimstone. He smells... like flowers."

"Since when does something so pure travel so far south. Well, your victim, I presume. Out for a game of lust tonight, demon?"

Joseph replies, "Uh... yeah. She was tasty. She was carrying tons of flowers with her. I just rubbed them all over."

"Doubtful. I bet you're just a little fairy demon aren't you. Obsessing of sinful delights? Why did you become a demon anyway? Couldn't get your fill?"

"I bet it just loves the prairie lands. Are you an angel lover, demon?"

Joseph retorts, "As in loving their flesh?"

"Doubtful. I bet he's soft like a baby's bottom. I bet those muscles are just full of.... meat... too."

"Yes, yes. Plenty of meat. Bet it falls right off the bone. No need to cook either."

Joseph makes an attempt at scorning them, "I'd be careful with your tone there, half-demon. I am made to rip your kind in half."

"Maybe with just one of us, and maybe behind the back, but we have the jump on you. Look at you. You can't even hold your ground. How did you claw your way out of the abyss anyway."

Benneth's voice carries from a shadow in the nearby tree, "Something like this."

Benneth leaps out of the shadow and buries one of his claws deep into the chest of the first half-demon. Joseph turns to the other half-demon who has already begun running and hollering behind the gates.

The half demon screeches, "ANGEL LOVER! AN ANGEL LOVER IS FEEDING ON DEMON BLOOD!"

Half demons and demons alike begin watching the half demon running down the street and mock him. A demon with bat's wings flies down from a rooftop and grabs on its shoulders. Another demon from the ground dives for its legs. The sheer force of the lift tears the half demon in half. The watchers begin to frenzy and feast on the entrails. After the body is consumed, they stare at Joseph and Benneth then continue on with their business.

Benneth explains to Joseph, "You're not going to like this, but we have to make our way to the castle, now. You will stall the King. I have to figure out what's happening to him."

"Happening to him? What did you do?"

"Call it a hunch. Trust me. I'll be in the shadows watching until you get there."

"How do I get there?"

"It's a straight shot to the center. You'll see it. Just run."

Benneth jumps back into the shadow.

"RUN!"

Joseph begins running through Dornar, as Benneth watches over him. Benneth notices that time is flowing much slower in the present, and watches as Joseph's sprint is more like a turtle running through a puddle of water. Even the demons were slower, much slower. This will be easy.

Benneth found that he had the opportunity to pick his targets well in advance. He would pop out and slay his victims with deadly precision, landing in another shadow to exit. They would not even have a moment to react. They would just fall below his blade.

Joseph's passage went easy, although very violent. As he ran, he bore witness to the sadistic and maniacal traits that separated the demons from the angels. He was not tempted in the slightest, but the sight was unlike any other. He peeled his eyes to his experience, and took in everything that he could.

The roads were made of cobbles, and as war torn as the surrounding buildings of basalt and obsidian. The fissure veins crossed the road many times, and bridges were built to cross them. The buildings appeared to be layers, as if the residents would continuously build over them as they crumbled. Many eras of this civilization were present. No two buildings looked alike. The streets were rank with demonic activity, many of them stumbling in overwhelming anger, and their aroma admitted their intoxication.

Many of them were sampling other forms of intoxication, whether they were herbs, pills, or even needles. The people were enthralled by provision the apothecaries sought to satisfy their hunger with. Although the sight was disturbing, it was depressing. There was little violence among the demons except violence against themselves. Visions of cannibalism were present as those who were present would feed on the fallen demons Benneth had been slaying. Demons could be seen overhead, watching, lingering among the rooftops, flying overhead. Joseph witnessed a subtle grace in their strides, even how they would extend their wings with shrill screams. It made Joseph think of his wings, and how pain is part of the demonic nature. He would feel this pain until the day he would be returned human.

Eventually they would make their way to the castle, and behold its eerie glory. The building stood ten stories high, and had the same feeling of layered architecture from eras of revision. The entire site had been made of the same obsidian and basalt combination, except it had been trimmed with gold and gems. From where they stand, it can be seen that any demon who dared steal from the keep had been slain, as their bodies had been lowered through the abdomen on tall wooden spikes reaching twenty feet high and reeking of decay. The keep itself had been surrounded by a massive wall, some three stories wide with the same level of architecture as the interior. The wall itself was mostly new, probably built in a recent area to expand its grounds.

Benneth, still being in the shadows, had been followed by the spectres the entire trip.

*****

King Nobelan seems to be enjoying his lunch on his throne today, and has a long table feast lying out before all the seats. His audience had been given intermission, and the doors are closed save for Adrian and Lorelei's entrance through the front door. Lorelei and Adrian immediately close the door behind them. The scribe also partakes in the feast.

Nobelan looks up toward his guests, "Oh! Adrian! Lorelei! Please, take your seats. Have lunch with me. We have much to discuss."

Lorelei's voice shakes, "Sire, we come bearing…"

Nobelan interrupts, "I know, I know. Dornar is a horrible place, something bad has happened. It always does. You seem dim, shaken even. You need food. Please, eat with me. We will discuss over lunch."

Adrian sighs, "Yes, my king."

Adrian and Lorelei take their seats and begin to eat, but appear to be barely keeping their food down.

"Is that making you feel better? Now, what is so dire that you insist on interrupting my lunch? Out with it, children."

Adrian mumbles to himself, "Funny because we are a few eons older…"

He then speaks up, "I mean, my King, dire news has reached its way to us from Moranda herself."

"I see that. Now what is it?"

Lorelei then informs, "King Rammathan is planning a surprise incursion with a full forced army."

"A WHAT?!?" Nobelan flips his plate over, "That filthy demon and his hot temper has really done it for him this time. If he tips the scales, the War Lock will surely plague us all. To think his own zealousness will lead him to kill his own people over the sight of angels on this planet. He is a buffoon and nothing more."

Adrian then advises, "My King, words do not save our people. We must take action, as soon as possible."

"And what of your friend, Joseph? Did he survive Moranda's inquiry?"

Lorelei answers, "He is fine. We confronted a chaosblood. Actually it was more like he was... waiting for us... He took Joseph with him to deal with King Rammathan. He claims to be able to slay him himself if need be."

"A chaosblood? Hah. Hah. Hah. So rich. Those weak offspring and their chaotic blood. Their bodies can barely keep the turmoil in their veins balanced. I'm surprised he's not rotting away at this minute."

Adrian corrects Nobelan, "This one is different, my King. He could... smell us. It was almost as if he was stronger in a way."

"Nonsense. Even if he was physically capable, his spirit could not be trusted. Too thirsty to be an angel, too pure to be a demon. Hah. Not even his human kind could accept him."

"He claims to have no human blood. He escaped Paradigm."

"Well, if he survives this incident, if we all survive this incident, you must bring him to me. Now, summon our offensive and ready the high guards. Adrian, you will lead them at the fields of the Blood Plains. They will die with their ancestors. Is that understood?"

"Yes, my king."

"Prove your stature to me and to your people. Survive this battle in blood and they will honor you. Now leave me to my lunch. You may eat at the barracks as you round the troops. This is dire, as you said."

Lorelei says, "I'm afraid so, my liege."

"Good. You almost upset my lunch here."

Lorelei and Adrian rise and exit the throne room. After exiting the court hall, they approach the barracks. There stands two criers at the sides of the main road in front of the courtyard leading to the barracks.

Adrian mutters to Lorelei, "More human than angel... more human... than angel."

"Don't be upset. He is preparing you. You will need this."

"That's not what I'm talking about. There's just something about him. It's not angelic."

"Don't worry about it. He's a good King. He has plenty on his plate."

Adrian calls out into the courtyard in front of the barracks, "Rally the offensive! Summon my high guard! Fall in!"

Two criers yell out with a voice that carries through the courtyard, "Rally the offensive! High Guard, fall in!"

Soldiers stop training and marching on a dime, turn and run in ranks toward Adrian, and form ranks ten paces out. They are all in many stages of preparedness. Some are wearing armour, some have been marching all day in light threads. All stand vigilant, sweat dripping from their brow and yet they do not move a single muscle.

The angelic High Guards circling the ivory tower soar down and fall in leading the soldiers. All of the High Guards don similar armour to that of Nobelan's, made of white jade and trimmed with gold and ivory. The armour is trimmed with silver and their scabbards are each uniquely plated with silver and gold overlaying carved mahoganies and cherries. Their shields sit low on their back, just below the joints of their wings, and made of the same woods and metals.

"My High Guard, I beseech you. Protect your King. Protect his courts. Save the lives of the weak and infirm. Today, we will be blanketed in darkness. Today, a demon threatens the flood plains."

The High Guard captain responds, "My Lord, we live to serve. Give us your will and your will be done."

"Take posts upon the castle and its gates. No demon shall breach its walls. Ready the defensive. All posts in all sectors. Summon the angels. All knights will be present on the outer walls. Call for Martial Law until the events subside. Gather all farmers. One the people of Elysica are gathered, lock the gates."

"Yes sir! High Guard! Move out!"

The High Guards return to the air and begin to soar in all directions with impeccable grace and resolve.

"My Offensive! There is an incursion on our doorstep! We march for the Blood Plains!"

The soldiers salute, "Aoo!"

*****

As Syrenne, Jennifer, and I approach the humble campgrounds of the Tribal Campgrounds, the people look at them with grim tidings. The land is scattered with various tents of the families of their council members. Children play in the tall grass as their mothers tend to their linens and prepare the foods. Only a few tradesmen are about, tending to nets and sharpening spears. A few of the others awaiting their Rite of Passage sit around the campfire having their faces painted. One master tent stands near the campfire, and is laced with bear's paw imprints and strands of sinew knotted with lynx teeth.

I ask Syrenne, "My people are upsetting me. Why are they upsetting me?"

"The day is upsetting us. The people are empathetic."

"I do tend to emit my empathy. We must play for them after."

"I would love to."

Jennifer smiles and says, "I'm looking forward to it."

They approach the council's tent. From its door flaps, smoke begins to bellow out.

Syrenne deduces, "This is either very good, or very bad."

I add, "And if it's very bad, we will make it very good." then rubs Syrenne's forearm.

Syrenne turns to Jennifer, "You should probably wait outside. It's for the safety of the future of the tribes that their identities remain secret."

Jennifer responds, "I understand. I'll just wait here and… play with my hair."

She notices a small cushioned bench next to the tent's door. The bench does not fit the scene and appears to be of the finest craftsmanship, the like made within Elysica. As she takes a seat, she finds it oddly comfortable.

"Before you go, can I ask you a question?"

I reply, "Of course, Jennifer, ask away."

"Back in the swamps. That Elysican. Why was she so far away from home?"

"She wasn't Elysican. She was a Dornarian."

"But, Dornarians are all so… 'grr', right?"

"Not true. They are the children of demons and humans. They themselves have not yet bathed in sin, and also have a human soul with the capacity for salvation, and choosing their path for themselves. Their parent's sin is not theirs, even if one of them was a demon."

Syrenne adds, "She was a light amidst the dark. Joy in a place of pain. They destroyed her for it."

"So very sad, and eye opening."

I explain, "Now you can see why justice must live in all places. Even in the refuse. These people can't just be segregated. They need to be loved."

Syrenne and Sorrownote enter the tent.

The tent's air is thick with pipe smoke. The five present council members sit around a small wooden cup, which seems to be generating the thin fog of smoke in the tent. The air seems to be slightly vented, enough to make the smoke not too unbearable, but noticeable. Gentle and ambient wisps of animal spirits form in the smoke. Animals are hunting other animals, grazing, etc. Yet again, Bear's paws line the walls of the interior. They appear freshly painted. Every so often, the footsteps of wisps appear in smoke smears on the walls, and the wisps paint themselves in, making impressions of the animals on the tent walls.

The tribe's representation includes a Bear's Paw, a Rabbit's Foot, an Eagle's Eye, A Stag's Horn and a Wolf's Howl. The rest of the council members must be the ones initiating the Rite of Passage.

The Wolf's Howl announces, "The council will now hear your plea, Sorrownote. May you enter a chord for us? It has been so long since we have had the pleasure of your company."

I take my seat on a cushion before the council members, and Syrenne sits next to him. I then pull out his lute from my cloak and begin to sing;

A Land of Order and a Land of Chaos,

Forever bound in parent conflict,

Must wage war once more,

 But all for naught, and their sons shall fall.

For a quarrel without due cause,

A petty indifference of a half just king,

A starving peoples whose fault is brought

By their own greed, jealousy and gall.

What must we do to stop this war?

But to fight once more, and die once more,

or settle before absolution is called.

I hail you now, brothers of the plains,

May we end this war before all is lost.

The Wolf's Howl responds, "We will answer your request, but on one term."

The Eagle's Eye says, "Where is the one made of light? Did you leave her beyond the tent?"

The Rabbit's Foot says, "I knew they would. I left a nice stool for her. Summon her in, Syrenne. Please."

Syrenne nods and exits the tent, then returns with Jennifer.

Jennifer coughs, "Oh. Hello. My, what thick smoke you have."

The Stag's Horn nods to Jennifer, "Welcome, child. What is your name?"

"Well, my name is JENNIFER. How can I be of service to you?"

The Eagle's Eye asks, "Are you in fact the one gifted with pure light?" and looks to the rest of the council members, "I can see it in her. It is true. Pure light. Astonishing."

"You can see it too? Apparently you're not the first one. Moranda said I was just human."

The Rabbit's Foot says, "Well, Jennifer. I know exactly what you are. I also know that your counterpart has been cursed by the darkness, has he not?"

"I wouldn't go saying he's my 'counterpart' but yes we are with him, he happens to be aiding the situation in Dornar."

"Oh, a naive child, but with potential. I just so happen to know exactly what it is you two are, but I am sorry in the fact that I may not tell you or it could damage the very fabric of what made it come to be. You will learn in time. In the meanwhile, I have a present for you, a gift unlike any in the land. Will you follow me? Let me hear the chime of your voice."

Jennifer opens up in a simple chord. Her voice lights up the world as if a dove has entered the room. The animals within the smoke stop and take audience, and birds begin to bellow out of the wooden cup. The song lifts all the pain from the world and all their hearts are lifted if only for a moment.

The Stag's Horn hands her a scroll.

"This is the gift, Jennifer. I have a scroll for you. Do not sing it, for the scroll will burn. Memorize it. Commit it to memory. Throw it down and sing it clear as the battle meets climax. Do not sing it a moment sooner, and only if a settlement is not reached. Go now, Minstrels. Make haste to the scene. My warriors will follow in due time."

Chapter 5

Joseph passes the first set of gates and enters into the castle grounds, and into the main courtyard. It appears to be next to vacant for some reason. From a corner, he sees Benneth's waving fist protruding from a shadow. He approaches him.

Benneth whispers to him, "Whatever you do, you cannot let them know I'm here. You must demand an audience. You have to be staunch and arrogant about it. Stand taller than your position. Show some pride. Buy me time."

"What are you going to do?"

"I can't tell you why, but I have a feeling this is not the king's doing."

"Okay, I guess. Here we go."

Two elites happen to be standing before the gates to the inner courtyard. One of the large demons, obviously one of Rammathan's Elites bearing mighty obsidian plate covered in gold spikes and wielding a great axe made of wrought iron takes note of Joseph, standing in the corner and talking to himself.

"You, there! Why are you talking to a wall?"

Benneth whispers to Joseph, "Act delusional."

Joseph slurs out his words, "And another thing! I just plain don't like your face. It looks like your mother kissed a mule."

"Right, then. Be on your way! All the demons are marching for Elysica. Why are you straggling behind?" the demon lowers his axe and pulls a whip from his belt, "Do I need to beat sense into you?"

Joseph reels his head around and deepens his voice with a guttural tremble, "If I wanted your opinion or your demands I would have asked for it. I dare you to crack that whip, so I can take it from you and hang you with it."

The second Elite looks and notices Joseph, "Ah. I see a commoner would like to have audience with the king. It is such a pity that I haven't had my lunch today. The fresh flesh will serve as a great addition to my feast."

The first Elite moves to stand between Joseph and the other elite and scorns him, "This straggler is a fresh meal for King Rammathan himself. When was the last time you saw a fresh meal walk to his plate? I should end you now for even considering him your own!"

Without fair warning, the Elite unleashes on his partner, raising his axe and nailing him across the chest. He then proceeds to pin him to the ground and tear into him with his great obsidian claws. The hungry and fallen Elite roars and flails his arms at the dominating Elite's face, exposing bone with every scratch. The two Elites begin tearing each other limb from limb and feasting on each other's flesh.

Joseph stands watching in stupefaction.

He stands over the now flailing Elites and announces with his chest out, "I remained behind to speak to the King. I have no time for your pathetic gestures. An insignificant cur has no place in the political theatre. Now grant me access to the King or I will tear you apart and send you back to the abyss myself... hello?"

Joseph steps toward the gate and opens it, at which point it appears the Elites have forgotten his very existence and are pleased with their meal. Beyond this, the site is gruesome.

Benneth returns to the shadow, where he stands before fallen and rusted gates. The Spectres stand there waiting for him.

Jennifer's spectre says, "There's something in there."

Adrian's spectre says. "I'm afraid we cannot follow."

Syrenne's spectre says, "Your answer lies inside."

Benneth is slightly irritated by their synchronized response and shakes his head, "I get it. My mission. It's ok. Understood."

My spectre says, "It's not that. We are powerless to change our fates. You still live."

"Oh. Gotcha."

Benneth passes through the mangled and rusted gates and beholds piles of corpses riddled with rot and giving off an unholy stench that fills the air. Great demons trudge among smaller demons which stand in formation, and although their stature implies gargantuan strength and power, they are withered to the bone, starved and diseased. Even the great beasts that line the walls and sit next to the piles of corpses have given up in their exhaustion and refuse to eat the rotting corpses. Benneth drapes his cloak over his face and continues forward to the main keep doors. The doors swivel forward with a spine tingling screech.

More spectres line the room, walking randomly and carrying on in murmurs of unintelligible sounds carrying a faint resemblance to discussion. Looking forward, the throe remains empty. Rammathan is nowhere in sight. Even a trace of a larger, withered demon is nowhere to be found.

The sound of cackling resonates from behind the throne.

Benneth finds a door, and slowly swings it open. The room is appears to be a personal study and war room, with bookshelves against the surrounding walls a large desk off to the side. A large table of stone rests in the middle of the room. A Mechanoid is strapped to this stone table, and is surrounded by coins and chalices of wine. Three demons are pulling on the flesh of the Mechanoid in chunks, but the flesh rejuvenates itself as they pull and vanishes into thin air as they attempt to devour without mouths. They also raise the chalices of wine to drink but the wine never escapes. The demons and the Mechanoid are riddled with plague scars and also appear to be starved.

Benneth draws his blades prepared for combat, enters the room, and yet the three demons are completely absorbed in their conquest, and ignore his presence.

The Mechanoid says, "I was wondering when you would show up."

"Wait. What?"

"Show up. Enter. Arrive."

Benneth is puzzled yet again, "I got that. How have I become so popular?"

""Unlike these miserable saps, I've been waiting here since the world ended. Oh it was a task, switching my circuits to wait for a 'change in environment' sort of speak. Yes, I'm being eaten alive, but I assure you, I feel no pain."

"Why would you want to wait for something?"

"Tell me now: If you were strapped to a table being feasted on for an eternity, wouldn't you like to awake for that single moment in time that could be you escape?"

"I'm starting to get you. It must be the robot side. So you're from Mechanus, aren't you?"

"Unfortunately. I was sent to give these buffoons an elixir. I'm afraid all of this is my fault."

"Sent? By whom?"

"These gluttons. So, what brings you here? Can you get me off this table? You don't appear to be a shade like these."

"Well, that's because I'm still alive. I guess you're what I'm looking for."

"I'll tell you what. Giving that guy this elixir is my big mistake. If you can turn this around, this is what needs to be turned."

"Sounds good. I thought I would have to dust for prints or something."

"No problem."

"Give me a second. I need to use a magic trick."

Benneth sticks his head through a shadow and peers into the present. He witnesses the tribunal of demons enjoying their feast laid before them. One of the demons has the head of an oxen, one of them a head of a panther, and the other a head of a snake.

The oxen headed demon speaks, "I feel my spilling of hate for Nobelan has made a climax with Rammathan. He will slay him on the field, at least if Nobelan is proven weak. If not, Rammathan will be slain and we will be made Kings!"

The panther's headed demon adds, "My deceit has left him believing our people starve. He will ravage their crops and we shall feed for many seasons to come!"

The snake's headed demon adds, "And my treachery has convinced him that his people are feasting on his possessions. They will prove their worth to him on The Blood Plains, and they will die for our victory! More shares for us!"

The oxen's head then leans over the Mechanoid and hugs its head, resting his cheek on its forehead. Tears roll down the Mechanoid's cheek and land on the table.

"And all thanks to you, Mechanoid, and your lovely little elixir. He can't keep his lips off the decanter. So naive for a KING."

The Mechanoid then speaks to the demon with a shake in its voice, "You have no idea what you're doing! King Rammathan will go too far! We'll all die! The War Lock will never let this happen."

The panther's head stares at the Mechanoid in wonder, "Who would've thought a blood cell of such a great organism like Mechanus could have such a loud mouth. You served our purpose, now feed our bellies!" and grabs a chunk of its leg. The Mechanoid recoils in horror.

Benneth, overwhelmed with anger, takes his opportunity to reveal himself and buries his blades into the oxen's head demon.

"I'm only going to need one of you. So who dies next?"

The oxen's head lowers himself to his knees as the others stand in shock, and begins pleading for his life, "Please! Anything but this! Anything but the pit! I just wanted my glories."

"I can't believe I share blood with your kind. Now this is what's going to happen."

Benneth turns and decapitates the snake's head.

*****

Joseph enters a series of gates which lead to the main courtyard. Within the courtyard, row upon row of demons stand fixed at attention, wearing plates of obsidian trimmed in wrought iron and gold. Larger demons patrol the lines, carrying whips tipped with spiked iron balls. One of the smaller demons begins to limp, and is pummeled to the ground. It then slowly regenerates and rises to its feet again. Ones that do not rise are tangled in the whip and tossed into a pile of bodies to the side, where dragon-like beasts rest and feed on the corpses. A few of them are still twitching, being the ones the beasts seem to prefer.

A straight path of cobbles down the center of the courtyard leads to the throne room. Through his march, Joseph remains uninterrupted by his surroundings Ones who sneer at him are whipped and punished. The giant demons themselves pay no attention to his march, watching in anticipation and hoping that one of their soldiers will fall out of line.

As he enters the throne room, he is surprised to see no great demons among the occupants. Those who reside within the throne room are simply acolytes and warlocks praising their governing demons and squabbling over petty differences, plotting behind each other, bartering slaves, and making deals with foes of foes. Some of these deals ignite in passion and they fight to the death. One such fight leads to a demon tossing a human into the pit to the abyss, a great gaping hole before the throne of King Rammathan, with nine smaller thrones that have been cracked and clawed into rubble.

King Rammathan beckons Joseph, "Approach, young warrior, and I will make you a god among men."

Joseph replies, "I have no need for great riches, only your ear."

Rammathan imbibes directly from the decanter of milky black liquid in his left hand, and shouts, "Why must my food always speak? Can anyone answer me?"

The room grows silent and Joseph takes a step back.

With foam beginning to crawl out of the corners of Rammathan's mouth, he shouts again with a much more guttural tone, "Pitiful underlings and their murmurings! Have you nothing useful to say? Huh? You always go on with your own concerns. Your king has a question for you!"

Joseph mutters to himself, "Oh boy."

Rammathan picks up his battle hammer, which appears like a cinder block made of wrought iron and reinforced on the heads with multiple layers of thick iron sheets, with a demon's claw for a pommel at the end of a staff-long shaft. He puts his weight on it to rise to his feet, and launches it at a random acolyte. The acolyte folds around it as it sails into a wall. Its abdomen is crushed in the process, and is implanted into the wall face, stone crumbling to the ground. Eventually the body and the hammer falls. The body hasn't been severed in half, but might as well be.

Rammathan continues into a rant, "I should be AT THE HEAD OF MY INCURSION. Instead I am surrounded with melodramatic rabble and their petty indifferences. I WANT TO TASTE ANGEL BLOOD!"

He lets out a blood curdling howl.

"Tribunal, my decanter is empty again!"

Out walks Benneth, the oxen head pitchforked on one fist, the snake head pitchforked on the other, kicking the rear end of the squabbling remaining counsel as it crawls to the throne. The Mechanoid scurries from the room. Onlookers mock the Mechanoid as he escapes.

Benneth shakes the heads loose at Rammathan's feet.

Rammathan shouts, "A Chaosblood in my courtroom? Guards!"

Benneth explains, 'We killed them, too. Well... they killed each other... well... I won't go any further..." as a shiver rolls up his spine.

"You must pay for your insolence!"

Benneth stares Rammathan down and approaches his throne in stance with his blades forward and orders him, "Sit your royal ass down and listen to what this piece of trash has to say." Then looks toward the looks at the counsel and orders it, "Spill your guts or I will spill them for you. Right here, on this cold, stone floor."

"My master, we only wanted to advance your kingdom."

"I smell betrayal! Betrayal!"

Benneth is now standing before Rammathan, with a foot on his throne and between his legs and a blade at his throat, "King Rammathan, your anger and hate does not benefit this discussion in any way. Drink this." He then tilts his other weapon back and allows the vial to fall into Rammathan's lap.

"How can I trust you?"

Benneth mocks his long, wolf-like snout, "Give me a break, with a nose like that? Just sniff it. Your own tribunal betrayed you. I brought them to your feet."

Rammathan begins to shout, "How dare you..."

Benneth interrupts, "Drink!" and turns around to kick the counsel in the head as it grovels at his feet.

Rammathan drinks the contents of the vial, and begins reeling his head back and forth as he is overcome by its toxin his eyes squinting in the pain it brings, muttering, "Reason. How I hate reason. I feel... conscience overcoming me. What an awful feeling."

"These idiots were poisoning you. They wanted you to start this war. Where is your army?"

"I have sent my front line. You're too late" Rammathan tries to speak as he cackles, "You have nothing to worry. I can see how all our fates could have been jeopardized. My real army is out front in the courtyard preparing. I will send them on each other for my amusement. Good luck, and don't get eaten on the way out!"

Joseph pulls Benneth away from the throne, "No need. Run!"

Joseph and Benneth run for the door as the acolytes begin to close in on them. As they exit the building, the demons on the doorstep stand watching, licking their jowls. Joseph lets out a blood curdling roar as he uses all his strength to force his wings out of his back sending slight streams of blood through the air in the process. He then wraps his arms around Benneth's chest and launches upward, far into the sky and beyond the cloud that hangs over the swamp. Elysica is visible in the clear air, a single beacon of light directly north of the shadowed swamp and beyond the plains.

As Joseph begins flying toward Elysica, Benneth tucks in his arms and legs, watching the land below pass them.

Benneth asks, "Wings, huh? When did you figure that one out?"

"At the beginning, actually. I've just been saving them."

"Did it hurt?"

"I think I got used to it, like it's a part of me. Seeing those demons back there, it's awful, but I got to see how they move. How they live. It all makes sense, in a dark and despairing sort of way."

"Yeah. Demons. I understand it but I'll never get it. I guess that's the angel in me."

"We were pretty gruesome back there. I hope it never takes hold."

"I take it as it comes. We need to get to the front."

"Got it."

As Joseph begins to dart forward to pass the swamps, they witness hordes of demons and half demons pouring out from the tree line. They are running across the plains, either mounted on beasts or running on all fours. They join a much more massive legion of forces, forming ranks. Their ranks appear to fight amongst themselves.

Joseph turns his head to see a swarm of demons flying behind him.

Benneth looks up to him, "Just drop me. I can take care of myself."

"Are you sure?"

"Just do it!"

Joseph drops Benneth. Benneth begins steering himself through the sky and lands in the shadows of a demon's beastly mount, disappearing into the End of Time.

Unfortunately for Joseph, the swarm surrounds him and rakes at his flesh. Fighting in the sky is unusual to him and he begins to tumble through the air and grappling with any demon getting close enough, but it makes no difference. He is one, and they are many. His rage and despair takes over, and in that moment he begins to feel stronger. The light around him begins to bend inward with the gravity of his emotion. He pulls his wings in and attempts to regain his balance, flares his wings out and buffets himself forward with all of his strength. He breaks through the swarm, sending demons spinning through the air and rockets to the Elysican front lines.

A flying angel in full white jade armour reflecting the status of a captain halts Joseph.

"Quick, Joseph! We'll hold them off!"

The head of demonic swarm begins to gain ground, with a captain leading them.

"We will feast on your flesh soon enough, angel!"

The head of the swarm stops in their tracks and begin cackling among each other, then return to their lines.

The Captain rests his hand on Joseph's shoulder.

"You're lucky we can tell you apart."

"What do you mean?"

"A demon is a demon, but you. It's almost like the light was bending and you were absorbing it. I've never seen that before."

"Really? Sweet."

"Adrian and Lorelei are below, at the head of the army. They're expecting you."

"Thanks."

Chapter 6

Joseph takes a second to peer down toward Adrian and Lorelei. He spins himself in the air with his wings, then pulls them in and rolls into a dive toward the ground. At the last second, he flares his wings out sending dust and dirt in all directions, revealing himself landed on one knee. He had aimed his landing perfectly, right before Adrian and Lorelei, who are coughing and dusting their armour.

Adrian exclaims, "Joseph! You made it? How many more are coming? This can't be their entire force."

"This should be it. We solved the problem. King Rammathan was being poisoned. They were pushing him over the limit. He would've killed everyone."

"Good God. Well, at least there is hope for victory now. Those demons, with the right motivation they'll never give up."

"We still have a fight on our hands. I've seen these things. They feed on violence, even if they're told to go home. They crave "angel flesh""

"Well, they won't get satisfaction this day. It pains me to have to slay so many of them, but it must be done for the sake of Elysica."

Benneth leaps out of the shadow of a nearby warhorse and runs over to confront. He is winded and panting, blood caked to his fists

He takes a gasping breath to speak, "You have no idea what's going on over there. They've been starved for days. They're practically feeding off each other. This isn't a battle, or a war. It's feeding frenzy."

"We'll have to put them down." Lorelei asks with tears rolling down her cheeks, "Are there Dornarians with them?"

"I'm afraid so, but they can barely hold their ground. The demons are picking them off like apples."

Lorelei shudders.

"Let's end this swiftly. I'll take command of the archers. I brought my own wolves along."

She puts her index fingers into her mouth and whistles loudly, enough to carry across the plains. From all corners of the army, well over a hundred wolves begin to weave through the soldiers, standing anywhere from hip to shoulder height and stocked as bears. They begin to take formation at the head of the army. One of the greatest of all the wolves, a massive white wolf runs forward, reels around and stops before Lorelei. The wolf lowers its head to the ground before her.

"They can smell their fate, but they are as defensive as we are of Elysica. They will make us proud."

She scratches the white wolf behind the ears, who growls in response and begins to pant. The white wolf then leaves to stand before the rest of the wolf regiment.

"Joseph, please stand with the footmen. They will need you."

Joseph recedes to join the footmen.

Adrian calls out, "Ready positions!"

The Elysican Army begins taking battle formations. The army's heart is led by the strongest of half-angel Elysican footmen and soldiers bearing pikes and sheathed swords and shields, and forms a semicircle. They lead in front of the human soldiers and militia, all wearing leathers and chainmail, donning swords and axes. To either side, a rear flank forms three rows of twenty ballistae. The ballistae are led by several rows of Elysican archers. To the far flanks and stretching for a mile stand two rows of Elysican Knights. Flying angels in full armor hover over the entire span of the army, watching over them and looking onward into the Dornarian swarm.

As the Elysican Army takes their ready, so does the Dornarian army.

They have no strategy or refined formation. Their army thrives on chaos and its howls and screeches can be heard over the distance. Unlike the Elysicans, The Dornarians are massed upon each other as a swarm of despair, feeding on each other and growing every minute with fresh soldiers from the swamp. Their flying demons swoop from above, picking up victims and fighting over them midair, tearing them apart.

Within the swarm, elites break through the front, tossing demons and half demons aside with their malicious and sadistic weapons. They begin marching across the field. The same darkness that hovers over the swamp seems to drift behind their leader as he walks across the field, and the elites intentionally walk in its wake, gathering strength from the trail.

The leader is one massive demon, wearing plates of layered obsidian trimmed with filigreed wrought iron and studded with thorny spikes. Around his neck, his chainmail reveals a bundled, scarlet velvet coif. His face is of a jackal and has been shredded by a series of raking marks delivered by various beasts. Numerous earrings hang from its elongated ears. Its gauntlets are plated with gold and in its hands it wields two shamshirs with a series of oddly cresting, bladed spikes running down their spines. The blades are dulled and have been sharpened by mallet alone leaving dents and chips resembling an uneven and tearing serrated blade. There are no scabbards on the beast's sides, and judging by its posture it moves as if it held the blades its entire life.

Adrian and Lorelei, slightly intimidated by the sight, call down several of the flying Elysican Knights, ones would have been High Guard and are of pure blood but chose to rally the offensive. They bathe in the light of the tower daily, and emit a light of their own that is reflected in their white jade armour. Their swords are of the finest and most precise of craftsmanship, almost as precise and quick as their resolve. Their presence seems to magnify Adrian and Lorelei's, bestowing the strength of the heavens. Two of the Elysican Knights within the cavalry ride forward and offer their horses. The flying knights hover over Adrian and Lorelei as they ride forward.

The demon and his elites halt midfield. The Elysicans approach.

Adrian orders with dominance. "Turn your army around. Your king is not behind you. He has already withdrawn."

"King? You think this is about kings? Our king sits fat on his throne. We are here for your flesh, angel. We have come to feed upon you. There will be no mercy today, only death, your death, and the death of all your kin."

"We give you fair warning. Turn around or meet your fate."

"Meat... That's the idea."

The elites watch as the large demon lunges at Adrian's horse and drives its shamshirs into either side of its neck. It then reels back its jowls and buries its teeth into the horse's nape. The horse attempts to free itself by bucking but the demon pulls it to the ground. At that moment, Adrian's knights lift him and Lorelei off their mounts and carry them to safety. Lorelei's horse runs back to the line.

After removing and gulping down a chunk of the horse's neck, the elites begin to feed on the remains. The demon turns to face his army and howls. The howl echoes across the plain and the swarm begins to charge the line.

Lorelei calls out, "Ballistae, Fire! Archers, Fire!"

The archers and ballistae loose a volley on the oncoming demons. The ballistae penetrate the swarm, impaling them by the dozen. The arrows are caught in the aerial swarm above, who begin to drop to the ground below. Many of them fall, but they continue to press forward.

Adrian and Lorelei run behind the front line of pike wielding footmen.

Adrian calls out, "Soldiers, shield Wall!"

They brace their pikes as they draw their shields to form a front crest surrounding the soldiers.

"Press forward march!"

Lorelei stays behind with the archers and ballistae as the front line with its militia and trailing soldiers begin to march forward, with the wolves taking the lead.

The Flying captain calls out, "To battle!"

The entire flying angel battalion releases a thunderous battle cry over the land as they soar toward the demons, keeping pace with the wolves at the head.

Volleys continue to launch into the oncoming swarm, picking them off as they approach.

As they charge across the land, the wolves are the first to break the lines. Their beastly approach to combat meets the demons on the same keel, and they begin to rake at each other's flesh. The soldiers continue to press forward until the shield wall meets the demons. Combat ensues between sides. Only demons who the front lines deem weak enough are given the moment to break the line, only to be confronted by human soldiers and militia who end their lives without mercy but with a quick and painless resolve. Every strike of the Elysican army are delivered precisely, avoiding the agony of long drawn pain. Unfortunately for the Elysicans, the ones who fall are not met with a fair fate, being torn apart for food by the Dornarians.

Angels and demons overhead ensue in battle, and become a cloud of chaos radiating flashes of light and darkness as they perpetuate the eons old war between heaven and hell. Angels and demons alike fall from the sky into the combat below.

Joseph, standing among the footmen, takes every opportunity he can to deliver fatal blows to the attacking demons. The front lines notice his strength and begin feeding him more challenging opponents, bottle necking a line of adversaries who tempt fate. Joseph embraces his newly found gifts and shows no mercy.

Benneth can be seen, leaping from the abundant shadows provided by piles of corpses. He waits in the end of time, watching the floors like a series of springs filled with unsuspecting victims, waiting for only the most opportune moments to strike. He leaps into the present, taking lives in single blows and landing back within the shadow.

Lorelei slowly marches forward with her archers, who begin to pinpoint their targets with direct shots. The surviving wolves break the line and fortify their march, taking down demons who dare charge the archers.

After the sky begins to shine again with the absence of darkness, the angel knights begin to close in from above, preventing any escape.

Adrian cries out, "My cavalry flank!"

Adrian notices the massive demon, standing in the center of the remains of the swarm which still appear to be thick as night. He begins approaching slowly, mocking Adrian by muttering with his lips, "show me your power, future king."

Adrian's personal knights step aside at his command, and allow the massive demon to approach. They begin to duel. The massive demon's intensity and strength is overbearing, but Adrian's grace and sure footing proves to be a challenge. The battle continues around them unabated.

The Elysican knights charge forward and fold along the sides of the demons, delivering the absolute verdict by the tip of their blades.

A guttural bark can be heard from the edge of the swamp, and Dornarians atop the backs of massive lizards break the tree line. The cavalry pulls back to once again form their lines and turn to respond.

As the cavalry rushes the lizard riders, the Blood's Plain tribesmen arrive with Syrenne, Lorelei and I at the lead atop mustangs.

The tribal warriors begin chanting, and beating their spears on their shields as drums.

The demons, amidst the thick of their battle, turn and gaze upon the tribal warriors. They are frothing at the mouth.

Jennifer slowly trots toward the field of bloodied battle and corpses, then dismounts. Some of the demons try to run toward her, but the Elysican Knights run them down.

Jennifer's eyes well up as she beholds the carnage before her. Her wings flare out and an ambience surrounds her. She begins to walk through the heart of the battlefield unscathed. Even the demons entranced are witnessing her untouchable perfection, disgusted by the thought of harming her, allowing a single moment of this brilliance to last a lifetime. They stand humbled by her magnificence. Even the cavalry and lizard riders cease to fight as they behold her beauty.

Jennifer approaches the winded Adrian and his opponent who are still mid combat. As she approaches, they become exceedingly exhausted.

Standing before them, Jennifer begins singing a confounding song of pure beauty and holiness that penetrates even the blackest corners of the demons' hearts. As they listen to her song, Elysicans and Dornarians like become entranced, drop their witness, and cease to act except to behold the beauty of this single moment as a hub of their realities.

As the song becomes quiet, the soldiers turn to each other and cannot find a single feeling of hate or drive for violence. Not even their hunger can be satisfied by this carnage. Looking to their feet disgusts them. They lower their heads, turn their ways and begin marching home. The demons cease to fight among each other, not making a single sound as they trudge back into the swamps.

The massive demon, exhausted and kneeling, facing Adrian, whispers to him, "I will see you again soon, future king." He then stands to his feet and trudges behind his army.

The Elysicans are left in a maze of corpses littering the battlefield.

Chapter 7

Syrenne and I ride forward as the tribal warriors begin to sort and pile equipment from bodies. We then dismount and approach Jennifer.

I say to Jennifer, "Of all the songs, and all the poems. I will never amount to what you have done here today. Jennifer, you have one beautiful gift."

Syrenne then adds, "Please say you'll sing with us."

"Sorrownote, your songs are what make you who you are. Just because you've heard me sing doesn't give cause to give up on yourself. Please, keep writing. Syrenne, I'd love to sing for you. "

Jennifer hugs Syrenne. That is the moment when I decided to make this chronicle. With that being said, I wonder what would have been the moment I would have decided to write the chronicle that would lead to the War Lock's ascertaining of my writing, or even the level he had received it at for that matter. Who knows? What I do know is this. This chronicle had proven its worth in this moment and hopefully in the days to come. My long winded sorrowful bantering of a journal would now aspire to more. Unfortunately for Benneth, he probably has no idea that I am now writing this, or that I have read his passage.

I apologize, now on with the story.

Joseph steps forward, torn and exhausted from the heat of battle. Jennifer touches his wounds and he is healed, but then she looks into his eyes and is saddened.

"There's a wound inside your mind I can't heal, Joseph. I'm afraid. Please, don't let this form consume you."

"It's like I get enveloped in rage and anger. It feels so wrong, but it's so pure. I can't help it. But after, now, I just feel awful. What have I become?"

"This isn't you. We're going to fix this."

Jennifer lies her head against Joseph's chest as she embraces him.

"I know. I'll do my best. I'll do it for you."

"You need to do it for you."

Benneth appears out of the shadow of Jennifer's horse and begins walking toward her. As he approaches, he removes his mask for the first time. Joseph can't help but stare.

Jennifer looks surprised. "That is an interesting gift. You seem... unaltered."

"I'm half angel, remember. I know that voice. My mother had a voice like that. You were singing a song written in heaven. I took the queue. I've just been waiting for everyone to turn tail."

"I see."

Adrian then approaches Jennifer and informs her, "You may not know this and you may never will, but heaven has ambient voices like yours which trail off into the eternity. There is an entire choir among the angels who serve a sole purpose of singing. Benneth is right. Wherever you learned that song, that song was one of theirs."

"The Tribal Council gave it to her." I explain.

"No wonder. It must have been the peace offering given by Adira. That song is peace."

Lorelei adds, "Even the demons reacted to it. You may not know this, but demons were angels at one time, long ago. They wanted to be gods, and didn't want to spend eternity in servitude, and in rebellion they were cast out from the light into the darkness."

Syrenne wonders, "What worries me more is why this event has happened. What or who would do such a thing?"

"It appears fate itself is serving justice with a side of curiosity today. So... what happened to Rammathan?" I ask.

"He was being betrayed by his own tribunal." Benneth responds. "If it went their way, the War Lock would've probably culled the land in plague. Talk about a show stopper."

Joseph steps away from Jennifer and rubs his stomach. "I don't know about all of you, but I'm famished."

Adrian pats Joseph on the back. "I don't know if my wallet could survive you being 'famished' again. Let's convince the King to throw a party!"

Lorelei cheers in glee, "Oh I love parties!"

Joseph asks, "Hopefully with a large helping of feast?"

Adrian replies, "We'll whip something up."

Benneth rolls his eyes, "Yay. The King..."

Adrian puts his hands on Benneth's shoulders, saying "You'll be fine, Benneth. You held your weight today. He'll honour you."

"We'll see about that."

As we begin to walk from the scene, massive ox carts from Elysica arrive and the militia begins pulling the bodies onto them. Tears roll down their cheek as brothers, fathers and friends search for their loved ones among the maze of carnage. The Elysican Knights follow us on foot, bearing the flags of their families.

That evening, we arrive at Elysica. The citizens line the main road from the gates to the keep. Trumpeters are blasting tunes of victory that echo over all the land. Cannons shoot confetti and streamers into the air. The people applaud and cheer.

One spectator approaches us with a pack mule saddled with several empty baskets. As we walk down the main road, many more begin dropping gifts of food and rare goods into the baskets, patting and hugging us in the process. Children run from the crowds to follow us down the road, some with angel wings hovering overhead and watching in awe.

As we approach the courts, the front courtyard is filled with the surviving Elysican Knights. Many of them are bandaged and even so are standing at attention. One of the knights takes the mule by the reigns and guides it toward the kitchens. They salute us as we make our way down the corridor and enter the court hall. As we enter, they trail behind us.

Joseph looks to Lorelei and whispers, "So much for convincing."

"I was kind of looking forward to it. Adrian can be so 'convincing'."

"Hey, now, I have my moments."

Jennifer giggles.

As we enter the court halls, Benneth tries to slip in among the Elysican Knight ranks.

Nobelan stands from his throne with open arms and approaches, arms wide and hands facing palms up.

"Now you must tell me. How did you manage to stop the war from reaching absolution? My men have been sparing me the details for your return."

Adrian replies, "Well, the battle itself went as you may have predicted, but the outcome was found in our favour with thanks to Jennifer, for settling the field, and to Benneth, for finding the source of the incident."

Nobelan stops in his tracks short of a hug, and asks, "Benneth? And who is this Benneth?"

Benneth steps forward. "Benneth Aldercaine, sire. A chaosblood from Paradigm."

Nobelan flinches in response, muttering, "A chaosblood in my throne room. Ahem. Please, continue."

"I eavesdropped on King Rammathan's Tribunal to find they were poisoning him with a vial of Pure Hate distilled in Mechanus. A Mechanoid had delivered it to them. They were about to feast on him when I interrupted and exposed them to their King. Moranda gave me a Vial of Reason to get his ears even though he was drunk on hate."

"A chaosblood. I do not like this. Do not trust him, Adrian. He will turn on you at any whim. I thank you for your interest, Benneth, but please understand. Your kind cannot be trusted."

"My kind? I would not put your prejudice beyond you, King Nobelan. I will never call you my liege. You are not my king. You forced my mother to abandon me as a child to fend for myself in the most treacherous of domains and to this day you still place your mistrust in mere siring. Remember this day that I will once again save the lives of your kin before the true war is over, and you, yet again will prove how ungracious you can be.

Benneth recedes into the crowd of knights and slips into their shadows.

Nobelan sighs, "Well, that ruins the meal. I must learn to be more sensitive with my words around a chaosblood. You see what I mean? He leaves in a threat. He is a threat."

Lorelei steps in, "He was right, you know. You put such prejudice in mere genetics. He has been nothing but helpful since we met him."

Nobelan turns to Lorelei with a disciplining scowl, "And he will until the point where that help is dire and he will abandon you. Such is the way of chaos. Never rely on it for it cannot be trusted. Remember that. I do see that I hurt his feelings but some things have to be said and made clear, even to his own ears. Now what became of this Mechanoid?"

Joseph answers, "I recall a Mechanoid running from the room when Benneth walked out with the remaining counsel on its knees."

"See! Such actions befit a Mechanoid. Now we have no trace of a source."

Jennifer asks, "But what if the Mechanoid was a simple apothecary?"

"It is never that simple, especially in a war situation. It is now my position to send a unit to go searching for this Mechanoid, and to see why Mechanus has any business in Dornar. Will The Band take this calling?"

I nudge Syrenne and whisper to her, "Band. I like that. He has taste." I then face Nobelan and respond, "I will answer the call, my liege. I believe Ceris and Leona of Swiftarrow Outpost must have access to the mountains. They have gifts unlike any. I'm sure if the Mechanoid was trying to return to the Femur Mountains that would be his route."

So it has been decided. Enjoy the evening, for tomorrow, you set out on your new quest. Do not return until this matter is settled, and we shall feast on that day once again. Please, refrain from flight. We do not know what lurks beyond the Femur Mountains, and the last thing we need is for you to be preyed upon."

King Nobelan waves his advisor forward, who is porting a silver platter with a golden chalice of wine. He toasts to us, "To my brave and noble knights, the future king and queen, and their comrades, tonight we celebrate our victory!"

The knights cheer as King Nobelan drinks to the lees.

Later on that night, we sit on one of the tower's balconies, overlooking all of Elysica. The light of the tower has a strange way of penetrating the darkness, providing slight luminance across the plains. The streets are filled with festivities. We have our own festivities underway, with a banquet table filled with the finest foods in the land and several guests including nobles of Elysica, Belliscia and the Blood Plains. Clint is among them. Syrenne and I have been playing music, and in the off moment I have been attempting to obtain script from my new friends for the chronicles.

Joseph and Clint begin talking, Joseph embracing, saying, "It's good to see you, Clint."

"I told you we'd see each other again sooner than you expected. I knew you'd be back."

"Not out for business?"

"And miss a party with the saviours of Elysica? Right. Look. Eastport may be my home, but this is also my home. If you need someone to talk to, I'll be here. So, how are things with Jennifer?"

"You're not the first one to ask, that's for sure."

"Look at her. She's smiling at us." Clint waves at her, and she waves back. "You have nothing to worry about."

"I'm a demon. A BIG demon."

"Temporarily. Work on your heart. The rest will follow."

Adrian steps to the side, near a dark corner.

"I know you're there. Like you would miss a party like this."

*****

Benneth is standing on the balcony, but his attention is fixed on everything but the festivities. As he looks outward, he witnesses a completely altered ending. Elysica remains standing and there is no sign of plague. The situation is much stranger. The entire plains had been scraped flat to its limestone bedrock. Industrious machines continue to scrape at the earth and excavate in strip mines. The towns are all torn and asunder. The city itself has no life and is completely vacant, excepting shells of robots with absent presence. The spectres approach once more.

Syrenne's spectre asks, "Benneth? You are Benneth, right?"

"Yeah, we've been over this before. I'm Benneth."

Jennifer's spectre asks, "Before? Before what?"

"Seriously? Is this a game?"

Adrian spectre informs, "I'm pretty sure we've never met before. We have a scroll for you."

Benneth reveals his scroll. "I already have one"

My spectre then sighs, "Oh no. It's for worse. He has one."

Lorelei's spectre explains, "You have met us before. The War Lock told us you may have. This is bad."

"What's bad?"

Joseph explains, "Well, this means you're tied to this fate. If you solved the riddle, it should have been solved and the end of time would have carried on eons into the future. Your fate continues, though. I'm sorry, Benneth. It's only going to get worse."

Benneth reads the scroll.

"Oh no."

Benneth looks off into the distance and the Femur Mountains are gone. Only Mechanus and a single mountain stand in the distance.

*****

Benneth appears from the shadow and stares at Adrian, speaking with a strong sense of urgency, "Adrian, I can't tell you why, but we have to go."

Jennifer walks over and informs Benneth, "It is alright, Benneth. Nobelan retired. We all tried to smuggle leftovers to host a small party for ourselves. Check the table."

"I apologize for leaving so abruptly, but I cannot respect the man who banished me from my homeland over such simple coincidences."

"Don't worry about it." She smiles toward him.

Benneth goes to the table to find a collection of the finest foods and wines of the land. I pull out my lute, Syrenne brings out the panpipes, and Jennifer begins to sing a song. The rest of the night is enjoyed in peace and solitude.

Adrian walks over to the banquet table.

"We know. We're going to Mechanus in the morning to track down your Mechanoid."

"It's much, much worse than that."

*****

Made in the USA
Charleston, SC
19 May 2015